Aeris Legends 2:
The Dark Man's Wrath
A Prequel to Redeemer Chronicles

By Julie C. Gilbert

Love Science Fiction or Mystery?
Choose your adventure!

Visit: http://www.juliecgilbert.com/

For details on getting free ebooks.

Dedication:

To my friend Alycia, one of *River's Edge Ransom's* first readers.

Note to the Reader: You may want to read *River's Edge Ransom* and *The Huntsman and the Healer* first.

If you wish to jump right in, check out: What's Gone on Before.

Aeris maps available on request, please email
Devyaschildren@gmail.com

Table of Contents:

Who's Who and What's What:

Aeris – a planet created by Kailon

People Types:
Saroth – A people who live on the east side of Aeris's main continent. They are usually Gifted in the darker four of the seven magic schools and tend to become Destroyers, Shapeshifters, Conjurers, or Minders.
Arkonai – A people who live mainly in the northwest corner of Aeris's main continent. They are usually Gifted in the lighter three of the seven magic schools and tend to become Seekers, Guardians, or Healers.
Bereft – Majority of people on Aeris who have no access to magic.

Key Saroth:
Marina Castaloni-Saveron – former Destroyer, elder sister to Jackson and Gabriel, Daniel's wife
Jackson Castaloni – Conjurer, younger brother to Marina, older brother to Gabriel
Gabriel Castaloni – Shapeshifter (squirrel, wolf, beetle), younger brother to Jackson and Marina, loves Tielle
Antonio Castaloni – Marina's recently deceased father
Corabelle Castaloni – Conjurer, Marina's mother, non-voting member of the Tariku League
Gabriella Castaloni – Minder, adopted by the Castaloni family to fulfill the marriage contract with the Polani family
Marcus Polani – Minder, betrothed to Gabriella Castaloni
Tielle Toscano – Conjurer, loves Gabriel
Barsi – assassin for hire, works for Jackson

Key Arkonai:
Daniel Saveron – Huntsman, Seeker, Marina's husband
Raelyn Cordova – Healer, Marina's apprentice
Christa Lekros – Healer, friend to Daniel and Marina, Jordan's wife
Jordan Lekros – Guardian, Daniel's friend, Christa's Husband, Supreme Huntmaster

Other:

Kailon – Eternal King, Creator of Aeris

The Lady – immortal servant of Kailon

Dark Man – Jackson's master, a manifestation of the Outcast, an immortal who rebelled against Kailon

Key Locations: (maps available upon request)

Caramore – section of Aeris's main continent controlled by Saroth

Bastion – Arkonai capital city; seat of the High Council

Dominance – Saroth capital city; seat of the Tariku League

Aridel – Arkonai; located on the northwest side of Aeris's main continent

Temperance – neutral city; located in the center of Aeris's main continent

Outreach – neutral city; located on the southeast side of Aeris's main continent

River's Edge – Bereft village on the southwest side of Aeris's main continent; site of an old controversy surrounding Marina

What's Gone on Before?

Warning, contains spoilers for the works mentioned

In *River's Edge Ransom*, Jackson Castaloni forces his younger brother, Gabriel, to help him release a deadly disease upon the village of River's Edge. Next, he disguises himself as an Arkonai Huntmaster to hire Huntsman Seeker Daniel Saveron to kill his sister. Once Daniel discovers that Marina Castaloni is trying to save the villagers, he breaks his contract and helps her. Jackson promises Marina the cure in exchange for the sign of her birthright and her Destroyer Gifts. She pays the ransom, but Jackson tries to kill her anyway. Gabriel and Daniel fight Jackson. Gabriel's gravely wounded, but Marina uses some of her life energy and Daniel's to save her brother.

The Huntsman and the Healer picks up right after *River's Edge Ransom* and covers the odd courtship between Marina and Daniel. He fulfills a promise to Marina by escorting her to the Arkonai city of Aridel. When he returns to Bastion to explain himself, the High Council contracts Daniel to capture Marina for questioning in the River's Edge affair. To spare Marina the discomfort of prison, Daniel and his friend, Christa Arrington, make the arrest and move her to Christa's estate.

A cruel trick brings Marina out into the open where Christa's uncle, the Supreme Huntmaster at the time, arrests her. Marina spends several months in prison. Daniel visits often and questions her about Saroth life. Within the stark prison walls, their friendship deepens into genuine affection. A twist of fate has them fleeing the prison. They seek and receive a blessing from Marina's father shortly before his death. Their union is formalized by exchanging marriage vows at the Alamon Temple.

Prologue:
Big Secret

Lady Christa's Chambers, Soaring Oaks Estate, City of Aridel
Three years after the marriage of Marina and Daniel
"Welcome back to Shadow Oaks, milady," says Annie Kerns. The servant woman executes a perfect curtsy. "My mistress thanks ya for coming and apologizes for making ya wait. The master returned without much warning with several associates in tow. Lady Christa may be entertaining guests for a few more hours this evening, but she said she'd try to slip away if she can."

"Thank you, Annie," says Marina Castaloni-Saveron. She consciously stops herself from touching the servant's arm reassuringly. Despite many years in Arkonai society, she still has only a basic understanding of Bereft servants. They seem more skittish than the servants she grew up with. "It's been a long journey. I can spend a few hours resting."

Her last words may as well have been a bolt of lightning.

The servant woman straightens immediately.

"Would ye fancy a lie down?" she asks. "I changed the bedding meself this morning. The mistress said the entire room was at yer disposal."

"No, thank you. A chair will be enough," Marina assures the servant.

"I can have a bath prepared, if ya like," Annie presses.

"Tempting, but I think it best I await Christa's request in here," Marina replies. "May I use the washroom to rinse off?"

"As ya like, milady," answers Annie, gesturing to her left.

1

"There's a full washroom behind that curtain or there's a pitcher and a basin near the bed. I've already prepared some refreshments by the window. There's another hour of daylight yet, but once the sun sets, I'll need ta draw the night curtains."

"Would you like to eat with me?" Marina asks, trying to stave off another apology. "It's been a few years. I would love to hear what's happened in my absence."

The question prompts another curtsy.

"Beggin' yer pardon, but I need ta get back downstairs soon," says Annie. "Is there anything else ye require?"

"I could use a set of cards," Marina replies, hiding her disappointment behind a wry smile.

"The mistress thought ya might ask," says Annie. "I've placed a deck on the tea tray for ya."

"If you finish with your duties early, I'd love to play a few hands of Challenger with you, but don't worry on my behalf either way," says Marina. "I've had a lot of practice self-entertaining."

The servant's head bows, and she apologizes. This time, Marina can't stop herself. Sweeping forward, she seizes the woman's left hand with her good one and covers it with the damaged one. Although she can still use her right hand in most instances, the injury never fully healed, leaving her little to no feeling in her fingers.

"I appreciate your kindness, but I will truly be fine," says Marina. "Please let Lady Christa know where she can find me."

"As ya like," Annie says, dipping her head instinctively. Suddenly, she stiffens again and squeezes Marina's hand. Joy radiates from her eyes. "I almost forgot! When ye have had a chance to refresh, I'm ta take ya straight to the wee ones!"

"Wee ones?" Marina echoes. "I thought Lady Christa had a boy?"

"Aye, she did at that, ma'am," says Annie retrieving her hands. "He's as handsome as they come too. But he's not the only wee one. The mistress had twins."

After that shocking announcement, Annie leaves to attend to her other duties.

Somehow, Marina finds herself in the chair set out by the food. She stares blankly at the fine array of cheeses, bread, and meat, unable to do anything but let her thoughts race.

Twins. This must be the big secret she needs help with.

Trying to conceal the number of children born to the most

prominent Arkonai family in Aridel is utterly insane.

Does Jordan know?

Marina can't imagine him not knowing. The infants are almost six months old. Jordan's transition from Interim Supreme Huntmaster to fully functional Supreme Huntmaster of the Arkonai Hunting Guild had not been easy, but surely, the man took some time to see his growing family.

And I thought Saroth isolation customs were extreme.

Only the highest echelons of Saroth society clung tenaciously to isolation customs, which would hide the mother and new baby away for a month or two so they could bond properly.

"You should eat something."

The sound of Christa Lekros's light, almost musical Arkonai accent draws Marina up out of her seat and halfway across the room. She has enough time to consider—and reject—rules of polite society, but she manages to slow her approach enough to avoid completely knocking the lady over with her greeting. After a tight hug, Marina pulls back to observe her friend. They'd exchanged letters but not seen each other since Marina's unfortunate stay in Aridel's Northgate Prison over three years ago.

Christa's beauty hasn't diminished, but there's a strange combination of weariness, wariness, and cynicism in her green eyes.

"Tell me everything," Marina orders, guiding her friend over to the small table holding the untouched meal.

"You know most of it," Christa says, sitting on one of the chairs. "I got engaged. Over my protests, you weren't invited to the wedding. I got married. I had a lovely honeymoon with my new husband. Then, Jordan ascended to my uncle's position, and I ceased having any real use to society."

"That's not true," Marina protests. "You've done a lot of good. Daniel was raving about the new orphanage you set up last year in Bastion."

"That was a lot of fun," Christa admits. Her wistful expression melts into full regret. "But now even that's not *proper* or *safe* or *fitting* for a woman in my position. You know, I'm beginning to despise those words."

"What are you expected to do?" Marina wonders. "Stay at home and raise children?"

Marina didn't think it possible for her friend to look sadder, but tears suddenly well up in Christa's eyes.

"I wish," she whispers. Swiping at the tears, she sniffles a few times and collects herself. "That's why I called you here."

Getting up, Marina dodges the table and drops to her knees before her friend.

"What can I do?" she asks. The heavy weight of Christa's gaze settles across her shoulders.

"I'm keeping my daughter, Marina," Christa declares, "but I need your help to do it. Did you bring the Teleportation scrolls?"

"I did, but what do you need them for?" asks Marina.

"Jordan and I are leaving tomorrow for Bastion," Christa explains. "There's a welcoming ceremony at the Guild headquarters for our son. Morale's been low since Lord Asalor Ravine vanished with several huntsmen, huntmasters, and most of the Guild's funds."

"Daniel told me about that," says Marina. "He said Jordan wanted him to lead the efforts to find them, but that the task would be impossible."

"He's correct. Several Seekers went with Lord Ravine. Some have the skills to obscure their trail," says Christa. "They could be anywhere on Aeris. That's why the High Council is making such a big deal about the ceremony for our son. We'll be gone at least a week. I've arranged to leave my daughter with Annie's cousin. She had a boy shortly before my twins arrived, so she can care for her until I return. I need the Teleportation scrolls to deliver my daughter."

"Why do you look so sad?" Marina doesn't want to further hurt her friend, but she genuinely doesn't understand why Christa is keeping her daughter's existence a secret. "Does Jordan know about her?"

"No!" Christa places both hands on Marina's shoulders and squeezes hard. "And he can't find out."

"Why?" Marina tries and fails to keep the stunned question in. The One has not yet seen fit to bless her and Daniel with a child, but she can't imagine trying to keep such a thing from him. "He's her father."

Words flow quickly out of Christa.

"Arkonai society revolves around men," she explains. "The Guild is everything. When I return from Bastion, it will be without my husband or my son."

"But he's still a baby," Marina says, feeling dazed.

"He's also Jordan's heir and likely the next Supreme Huntmaster," says Christa, letting the words slip out reluctantly. "He belongs to the Guild, so he'll be raised by the Guild." Sighing, she stands and pulls Marina up. "Come, I want you to see them."

"I'm so sorry." Marina scrambles for something comforting to say as she follows her friend through the washroom into the adjacent chamber. "But if the Guild is only interested in males, surely they'd leave your daughter with you."

"For a few years, perhaps." Christa halts near two impressive cradles and picks up one of the tiny bundles. "Marina, I'd like you to meet Dina."

The baby reluctantly opens her eyes, regards Marina for a second, yawns, and leans back against her mother.

"She's perfect," Marina says, touching the infant's soft cheek.

"Yes, but there's also magic in her," says Christa, expression hardening with determination. "I've felt it, and I won't let it be wasted."

"Wouldn't she be trained as part of her education?" asks Marina.

"Only if she manifests an accepted school of magic," Christa answers, placing the baby in Marina's arms. "Even then, it will only be for show. She'll be trained to find a respectable match and little more." She stares at her daughter. "I can't do that to her."

"What are you going to do?" Marina shifts the baby into a more comfortable position.

"I'll raise her in secret," says Christa. "She'll have the best tutors money can buy. Arkonai, Saroth, or both if she wants."

"But Jordan—"

"He'll never know," says Christa. "He's hardly home, and when he comes home, he refuses to see me. It's part of a ridiculous vow meant to protect me."

"Won't somebody tell him?" Marina wonders. She moves the baby again to change the pressure on her arms.

"Few of the servants know, and besides, all of them came with the house. They're loyal to me."

Satisfied with the answers, Marina decides to help her friend with this mad scheme.

"Take her so I can get the scrolls for you," she instructs.

"I need to return to the dinner party soon, strange affair that it is," says Christa.

"What makes it strange?" Marina inquires.

"My own husband pretends I don't exist," Christa answers, frustration clear. "Seriously, there's a screen separating the two halves of the room." She sighs. "Forgive my complaints. When you grow weary of holding the baby, leave the scrolls and go in peace. I'll deliver her later tonight." Carefully, she wraps her arms around Marina's shoulders above the baby. "I know our ways seem strange to you, but this is what's best for her. Will you keep my secret?"

A solemn beat passes before the full implication sinks in. Marina won't be able to tell anybody, not even Daniel.

"You have my word. I will not tell a soul," Marina promises. "Would you like me to deliver her for you?"

"That is something I must do, but thank you," says Christa. "I've already put you in enough danger by summoning you here. And the fewer people who know of your involvement, the better."

Though Marina agrees with Christa, she longs to offer her friend more comfort. She settles for a momentary distraction.

"You said I could meet twins." She hefts the baby. "This is but one half of a beautiful set. May I see the other?"

Christa's worry fades as she picks up her son and holds him so Marina can get a good look.

"This is Devin. He came right after his sister, like a little shadow."

Chapter 1:
Right and Duty

Plains of Promise, Castaloni Estate near the City of Outreach
Three and a half years after the marriage of Marina and Daniel
(Christa's twins are about one year old)

"Today is a big day," comments Mika Forester. "Everything looks magnificent. You have quite the talent for this sort of work."

"Thank you, Master Forester," says Marina, aware each word could have far-reaching consequences for others. "Most of the credit belongs to the managers. I will pass along your compliments."

When we get a free moment to speak.

No guests have arrived yet, but they should step through the portal very soon. Personally, Marina thinks the expense of hiring a Portal Master for the occasion is wasteful, but Elena Polani—the groom's mother—had insisted.

"They may have done their parts well, but the success still belongs to you," Mika insists.

"I appreciate your support," Marina says carefully. "What can I do for you?" She can think of nine tasks that could use her attention, but clearly, the man won't go away until he says what's on his mind. As her father's long-time friend, counselor, and purser, Mika always voiced house interests.

"Your mother would like to speak with you," Mika says.

That catches Marina by surprise. She stops scanning the massive array of tables for problems and turns her full attention to the purser.

"I've not exactly been hiding," says Marina, trying to keep her tone neutral. "She knows where to find me."

"You know it's not that simple, Mari." Mika's tone pleads for understanding. Leaning closer, he lowers his voice. "You know what Jackson will do if she openly supports you."

Use of her father's nickname for her, stirs up sorrow and longing within Marina. She lets silence fall while her thoughts wander.

Likely the same thing he did to my father. Has it really been three years since his death?

The mourning period plus an additional two years to educate Gabriella in Castaloni family history and business affairs had delayed the wedding quite a while. The adoption was supposed to be in name only, but after Father's death, Marina's mother had secretly modified the terms adding Gabriella to the line of succession.

I guess huge secrets are more common than I thought.

Weariness lands heavily upon Marina's shoulders. The passage of several years has not dulled the pain of losing her father. She tries to distract herself by thinking of something happier, like Christa's twins.

They must be over a year old by now.

She has only managed a few clandestine meetings with Christa in the months since delivering the Teleportation scrolls, but each visit shows her the rapid growth of Dina.

The tactic works, lifting her mood for a few seconds, but the sight of Mika's patient smile pulls Marina's thoughts back on track. Knowing her brother, Jackson, caused Papa's death yet must remain unpunished, pains her.

Things have become quite complicated.

Her father's death left her sole heir of the vast Castaloni lands and businesses. However, Jackson's schemes have effectively ensured she can never return to Caramore, where most business headquarters are located. The regional managers have done their best to maintain things, but the lack of leadership has created many problems.

"You need to run the house council," Mika says, finally breaking the silence between them.

"Gabriel's kept me informed," says Marina.

"It's not enough," Mika argues. "He has no real authority, and the unrest is growing. I've done what I can to stall them, but if enough managers unite, they may successfully challenge Antonio's will."

"Would that really be so bad?" Marina wonders. They would be poorer, but she and Daniel barely use a fraction of the money set aside for her. Most of the funds sponsor the training of promising students, help establish new healing clinics, or provide loans to Saroth looking to set up businesses outside of Caramore.

"You know how succession works," Mika answers. "If you had a child, you could appoint Gabriel his or her guardian until the child gains the age of majority. He could run things in their name, but since you are of sound body and mind, it is your right and duty to assume the role yourself. If you lay down these rights, complete control goes to Jackson."

Marina tenses at Mika's last statement.

Unless Gabriella's willing to fight him for it. Does Mika know it's an option?

"Is there no other way?" She voices the question out of desperation, but she already knows the answer.

Mika only shakes his head.

"I know you have different dreams, Mari," says Mika, "but your people need you. Jackson's ambitions are intimidating, but can you imagine the harm he can do with the full might of the Castaloni wealth behind him? Your mother has a proposal for you to hear. Please, promise to at least think about it."

"I will speak with her," Marina promises.

"She is waiting in the gardens," says Mika. He rushes on before she can protest. "I can handle the affairs for the moment, and if it's truly important, I shall have somebody fetch you."

Stepping quickly, Marina picks her way through the maze of tables to the private gardens. Though the massive gardens hold many paths leading to quiet nooks, she knows precisely where to find her mother. Corabelle Castaloni's favorite spot has always been the main fountain right near the back entrance to the house. By the time she reaches her destination, Marina's short of breath. She pauses to gather her wits before facing her mother. She's seen her only a handful of times in the last several years and most of those conversations ended in disagreements.

Because she's approaching from the plains side, Marina sees her mother's back first. She's sitting on the fountain's edge, conjuring nuts to feed a small gray squirrel. The unguarded moment touches Marina. She'd forgotten about her mother's soft spot for squirrels since it's, one of Gabriel's forms. The three of them used to play catch with conjured nuts when Gabriel was a small child.

"Come and sit with me, Marina. We have little time and much

to discuss," calls her mother.

Pushing down an irrational feeling of guilt, Marina circles the fountain until she reaches her mother. A chair appears for her, so she sits and studies her mother. The stress has put a few more lines on her face and widened the gray streaks in her dark hair, but her cool expression betrays little emotion. Only a small but growing pile of neatly stacked nuts gives Marina a clue to her apprehension.

"Mika said you had a proposal to share," Marina says, hoping her mother will start the conversation.

"The time has come to take a more active role in the businesses." Stilling her hands, Corabelle levels a solemn stare at Marina. "Despite the provisions your father put in place, there are many people who will take advantage of managers not fully supported by the head of the house council. Ours is severely divided."

"That's not—"

"This isn't about blame," her mother interjects. "It's about this wedding."

"I don't understand," Marina admits. "The Polani name is more prominent than ours. I thought that was the point of this alliance."

"It is," says Corabelle. "The respect garnered by the name will open many opportunities, but we won't be able to take advantage of them without you. Many who run in the highest circles won't conduct business with people lacking full authority. That narrows the field to you."

"I can't enter Caramore," Marina says. Though it's not the first time revealing this fact, she still finds the admission painful. "Jackson made sure of that."

With a snap, her mother conjures a scroll and holds it out to her.

"I think I have a solution you'll find acceptable."

As Marina takes the scroll, the magic parchment transfers every detail of the contract contained within directly into her mind. Closing her eyes, she sorts through the key points. If Marina exerts her rights, the house council would establish a second headquarters in the city of Outreach. Although meetings would happen weekly, her obligation to attend and handle disputes would be limited to twice a month. In return, each of her personal ventures would be become part of the normal business. The first portion of the contract doesn't surprise her, the second part does.

"You added a death clause," she notes, torn between amusement and horror.

"The inclusion of one is not unusual, though the details might be considered so," says her mother.

Marina rereads the section swiftly.

"Has it ever been done?" she wonders. The contract covers the usual ground if she has a child before her death. The shocking portion only kicks in if Marina dies before having a child. In that case, her stakes transfer to her husband. "The managers are not going to like the possibility of control going to an Arkonai man."

Neither will Daniel for that matter.

She smiles at the mental image of her handsome husband decked out in his usual huntsman attire, standing before the Castaloni house council.

He'd rather hike through the Badlands without weapons, I'm sure.

"Then it becomes their best interest to keep you safe." The firmness in Corabelle's tone tugs Marina's attention back into place.

"Do you think I'm in danger?" she asks. Given her mother's extensive network of contacts, Marina has always respected Corabelle's instincts about such things.

"No more than usual," her mother admits. "Your choices— which I am not here to argue about—will always carry some danger from extremists on both sides, but you should be fine in Temperance. Will you sign the contract?"

"I'll have to speak with Daniel first," says Marina, "but the terms are fair, and I agree something needs to change. Gabriel's reports have told me as much. Shipments have disappeared. Suppliers have canceled contracts. Villagers have had their goods stolen soon after delivery. Little things mostly, but the number of incidents is worrisome. If I have the power to fix these problems, I will."

"You do have that power, my dear, but try to implement changes slowly," says her mother.

"What changes?" Marina asks.

Standing, her mother reaches down and touches Marina's left cheek.

"I know you," says Corabelle. "You've always had radical ideas. Some brilliant. Many frightening. Most will challenge long-held traditions and stir up hatred from many quarters." She lets her hand fall away from Marina's face. "Just give people a chance to adjust to changes. They'll come around once they see your methods work."

Until this moment, Marina had no idea how to protect the supply shipments from bandits, but her mother's words set off a cascade of thoughts. *The answer is so blatantly obvious,* she chuckles. Daniel had mentioned the Arkonai Hunting Guild's money woes. She could solve both problems. Huntsmen accepted protection jobs from Bereft villagers all the time, but villages often ran short on funds. Why was it such a leap to imagine huntsmen taking on the task of guarding shipments to villages?

The feeling of elation lasts several seconds before reality smothers it. There will be a lot of resistance from both sides. If she accepts her place as head of the house council, she can persuade them of the practicalities of such an arrangement. She'd get the scribes and counselors working on wording appropriate contracts. Getting huntsmen to take the contracts was a different matter entirely, one she'd need Daniel's help with.

And Gabriel.

The Arkonai Hunting Guild would not deal with her, but they might work with her husband and her brother.

"The wedding party and guests will arrive soon," says her mother. "You should get back to greet them."

Marina moves to follow the advice. The chair her mother conjured for her disappears.

"Jackson should arrive shortly as well," Corabelle comments. "He's been distant and moody lately. Will you try to make peace with him?"

Marina nods distractedly, but she knows far too much to put hope in the possibility. The urge to tell her mother everything puts a painful lump in her throat, but sense prevails. Confessing her brother's sins could get her entire family killed because of an archaic law about Unforgivable Crimes. One of her last promises to her father had been keeping Jackson's part in the poisoning secret. She didn't know if she'd ever forgive her brother for that, but she wouldn't endanger Mama and Gabriel to seek a hollow vengeance against Jackson.

Has he changed? Maybe peace is possible.

She hasn't seen him in years. Jackson tried to kill her at their last face-to-face meeting, but that was before the question of inheritance was fully settled. Once this new contract kicks in, her brother will have to accept the fact that he won't inherit the businesses outright.

Unless he destroys Daniel too.

Marina draws a few shallow breaths and desperately pushes that thought aside. The changes their father made before his death increased Jackson's allowance significantly, and that amount ties directly into the collective success of the holdings. She suspects her mother manipulated the allotments set aside for herself and Gabriel to appease Jackson. He should want Marina to succeed at keeping the businesses strong.

Only one way to find out.

Chapter 2:
The Proposal

Plains of Promise, Castaloni Estate near the City of Outreach
Same day

"You look like you'd rather be elsewhere," says Marcus Polani. "Truth be told, so would I, but I'm told I have several more hours of this meet-and-greet stuff." He sighs.

Daniel Saveron looks up at the sound of his friend's voice, then springs to his feet when Marcus's new wife emerges from behind him. Fixing his posture, Daniel tips his head in a partial bow first to Gabriella and then to Marcus.

"Lord and Lady Polani, I wish you—"

Daniel's formal well-wishes end in a rush of breath as Gabriella Polani throws her arms around his chest and squeezes tightly.

"We've missed you!" cries Gabriella. After a few heartbeats, she releases him and stands next to her husband.

"She's been doing that to everybody," Marcus says in response to Daniel's surprised expression. "Didn't think anything could catch you off guard, huntsman."

"He's not off guard, he's distracted," Gabriella says.

"And feeling out of place." Daniel peers past the couple to the hundreds of finely robed people. He'd missed Jordan and Christa's wedding since Marina couldn't attend, but he suspects even that paled in comparison to this one. Marina and her people have transformed the field into an elegant venue filled with thousands of flowers, beautiful linens, magical lanterns, and a spectacular fireworks display. "I've never been to a Saroth wedding before."

"Most weddings aren't this big, but my mother would consider nothing less," says Marcus.

"You love being the center of attention, and you know it," says Gabriella. Using Marcus's arm for leverage, she pulls herself up to tiptoes and plants a kiss on his cheek. "Now, tell Daniel the proposal. I'm going to see if his wife needs rescuing from our brother." With that announcement, she rushes off through the crowd.

The reminder that the Castaloni family adopted Gabriella to solidify the marriage alliance with Marcus's family makes Daniel feel like even more of an outsider. His people emphasize making a name for oneself through actions, but lands and possessions pass from father to son. That was Christa's problem when her parents died suddenly without a male heir. Women very rarely own property, especially in the upper echelons of Arkonai society. Everything Christa Arrington owned transferred to her husband and his name when she married. Daniel didn't know what would happen with Marcus and Gabriella, though he understood a very detailed contract had been established. The Saroth have a much more elaborate and rigid set of rules regarding the prominence of certain households. Marina had tried to explain it to him once but gave up when he distracted her with a back massage.

"What's on your mind?" Marcus asks, settling onto the seat to Daniel's right.

"Nothing much. Just thinking about the differences between our cultures," Daniel answers, also resuming his seat. "What's on *your* mind? Gabriella mentioned a proposal."

Marcus laughs and pours some wine for himself before topping off Daniel's glass.

"Are all Arkonai as direct as you?" he asks.

"You're avoiding the issue," says Daniel. Picking up his glass he salutes Marcus and drinks some of the pale-yellow liquid before continuing. "Given that it's your wedding, you can do as you like, but it looks like your time may not be your own soon." He nods over Marcus's shoulder where several people have gathered a respectful distance away.

Glancing back, Marcus waves for the people to wait before turning back to Daniel.

"I'm sorry. I thought we'd have more time, so I could explain better," says Marcus. "I believe we should work together."

"To do what?" Daniel asks cautiously.

"To combine the abilities of a Seeker and a Minder," Marcus answers. "As a Minder, I am very good at questioning people, but I can't see a room's history like you can. As a Seeker, you can see these things others cannot, but you also cannot share them as testimony like I can with a Vision Cast."

"I can only see a room's history under certain conditions," Daniel cautions. "And you passed out during the first and only Vision Cast I've witnessed."

"It is physically demanding work," Marcus concedes, "but I've been practicing with Gabriella for a few years now. We've gotten much better at it. I rarely pass out."

One in every four or five sessions is a bit more than *rarely*, my love.

Daniel hears Gabriella's thought as words inside his head, as if she stands right beside him. He knows the words are directed at his companion, but they amuse him anyway.

"How would this work? When do you need an answer by? Where would I go?" Several more questions tangle themselves inside Daniel's head, but he holds them back so Marcus can address the initial ones.

Come and greet guests with me. I will answer some of Daniel's questions while you do so. I'm better at multi-tasking, and they're mostly your family members anyway. There's only so much smiling and nodding I can do here without looking ridiculous.

"If you'll excuse me, I am being summoned elsewhere," says Marcus, "but I leave you in good hands. You can ask your questions in your mind for Gabriella to read or you can speak them softly, but you may wish to face away from the crowd to avoid looking odd." Marcus's eyes shine with amusement as he exits the chair and bows in farewell.

Before Daniel can reply, Marcus walks over to the growing cluster of people waiting for him.

"Do you need me to repeat the questions, my lady?" asks Daniel.

I remember them, but please, call me by my given name. You are my brother in the eyes of Saroth law, and besides, we have more in common than you know.

"Like what?" Daniel wonders.

We both fell in love with people far above our stations.

You are Arkonai, and I was the daughter of tenant farmers. We—and those we gave our hearts to—also want to see this age-old nonsense of distrust and animosity between the two magic races resolved completely.

"What do you require of me?" Daniel asks, inserting formality because it gives him a few extra seconds to process.

Gabriella's thoughts flow swiftly, though she delivers the words at something closer to normal speech patterns this time.

As Marcus said, you have skills we do not, and we have skills you do not. Our hope is that by demonstrating that good can come of working together, we may encourage the Arkonai High Council and the Tariku League to open fruitful discussions that will benefit everybody.

Picking up the neglected wine glass, Daniel holds it close to his mouth to conceal his broad smile.

"I am convinced you are passionate about this, but I should speak with Marina first," says Daniel.

It was her idea. Do not be alarmed that you are the last to know. It occurred to her about half an hour ago, shortly after a discussion with her mother. Marina still has much to do with making this party run smoothly, but she wanted you to be able to think about it because you must present the idea to your Council.

With effort, Daniel keeps his features impassive, but the idea makes his stomach muscles tighten. He takes several sizeable gulps of wine, then stares deeply into the remaining liquid.

I'm not on the best terms with the High Council.

But they will listen to you. Once you gain their permission, Marcus and Lady Corabelle Castaloni can present the proposal to the Tariku League. Your presence may be required at such a meeting, and Marina, Marcus, and I are willing to answer a summons should your Council require it.

"I'm not letting the Council anywhere near Marina," Daniel declares. Quickly, he sets the wine glass down so his hands can form fists without shattering the glass.

Politics had prompted Christa's uncle—the former Supreme Huntmaster—to imprison Marina for several months. The High Council had pretended to be investigating the tragedy at River's Edge, but really, they wanted to see how the Tariku League would react to the move. Despite the Council's official pardon, which cleared Marina of any wrongdoing, Daniel's trust in them remains shaken. Within the walls of the Northgate Prison in Aridel, Daniel's fondness for Marina had blossomed into a deep and abiding love for her.

They will not harm her again.

Peace, Daniel. Marina knows the risks and your fears and will honor any decision you make in that regard. I only wanted you to know she is as committed as we are to taking risks to obtain a lasting peace.

"Is peace possible?" Daniel asks.

We will never know if we do not try. To answer your earlier questions, you have what time you need, but we cannot move the plan forward without you. The first task will involve obtaining permission from both councils. To make this more appealing to the High Council, we would like to pursue those who raided the treasury in Bastion.

"You don't believe in starting small," Daniel comments.

Likely they will demand several demonstrations in order to build trust, but both councils need to see that combined magical talents can prevail where single ones cannot. The specifics of the mechanics will vary based on the task objectives, but in short, you and Marcus will investigate while I hide nearby and lend my husband the necessary mental support.

"I need some time to think," says Daniel.

Will this endanger Marina?

I shall leave you alone with your thoughts soon, but this is only one mutually beneficial idea Marina posed to us. To alleviate some of the Guild's financial troubles and protect Castaloni Shipping interests, she thought it might be prudent to hire huntsmen as escorts for certain caravans. Will you handle appropriate inquiries for her?

"I don't really have a choice about it," Daniel notes, suppressing a groan. "She'll march right into Bastion and demand to see Jordan if I don't."

If not that, then something as equally bold and dangerous, yes.

"I will make the request," Daniel promises. "It's not a perfect answer, and many will resist working for Saroth. But it may buy us some time. The theft is more serious than the High Council will admit. We need to do something soon, or there will be trouble."

Forgive my ignorance. I am not aware of how the Guild works. How will the treasury theft create trouble? You sound concerned.

"There are too many huntsmen and not enough paying jobs right now," Daniel explains. "That's not unusual. Lucrative contracts come and go, but in the past, the Guild could weather such seasons by using treasury funds to send huntsmen on mercy missions to remote Bereft villages. Without the funds, it's much harder to justify the risks."

Could they call for volunteers?

"They do, but some who would go must take smaller jobs to feed their families," says Daniel. "Idle huntsmen are dangerous. People are looking for something to blame. It's making radical factions like the Resolute and the Arkonai Brotherhood more appealing."

This would be a lot simpler if we could pay the debt, but the figure I heard was far more than the combined wealth of both the Castaloni and Polani houses.

"The High Council would never accept Saroth help anyway." Daniel's tone lacks bitterness until he voices a second statement. "Honor would forbid it."

Then we will find that money, with or without permission from our governing bodies.

"Let's ... try asking first," says Daniel. He fully believes Gabriella's promise, but the mission will be dangerous enough if they have permission to undertake it. Absently, he finishes the wine and stares into the empty glass.

We must hurry. The marks on the money will not last forever.

"How do you know that?" Daniel can't hold the question back, though part of him already knows the answer.

When we are connected like this, your surface thoughts become very easy to follow. I will teach you how to prevent that when we have time. I must go now but think about where we should begin the search.

A subtle shift within Daniel tells him Gabriella's presence has left his mind. He hadn't sensed her arrival, but the absence feels like a fleeting memory of wind brushing his face. While he doesn't mind the contact, he's aware that most Arkonai will fear it greatly.

Where did we get the idea that Minders are dangerous?

With nobody to answer his silent question, Daniel lets it slip away and turns his thoughts to finding Lord Asalor Ravine, his followers, and the stolen money. They could be anywhere on the western half of the continent, depending on the skill level of the Seekers concealing and removing the marks. Not every coin would bear a complicated mark but finding those that do would be time consuming.

What happens if we fail? It's already been a year. We have maybe two to three more years before they scatter forever.

The thought terrifies Daniel. Getting Jordan to give him the contract he initially rejected would be easy enough, but they would be collectively making some bold promises. Failing at the task could damage the hopes of healing the rifts between the magic races. Glancing around at the other wedding guests, Daniel is acutely aware of being the only Arkonai in attendance.

Things must change. We were never meant to be this divided.

Chapter 3:
Problems and Prophecy

Plains of Promise, Castaloni Estate near the City of Outreach
Same day
Gabriella and Marcus may be trouble, but the problems are all present, Master. Let me destroy them for you.

I agree the list of enemies has grown by two today, but if we are to conquer Aeris together, I need you to be innocent of their blood, at least by appearances.

Yet another half-drunk well-wisher stumbles toward Jackson Castaloni and opens his arms wide for a celebratory embrace. With a practiced move, Jackson seizes the man's arm and directs him onto the nearest empty chair. Next, he grabs a new wine glass, fills it, and presses it into the man's hands before retreating a few steps to think. He's been fending off similar attacks this entire evening.

Could you intervene? He's only partially joking. *Nobody could blame me if a convenient, tragic accident suddenly consumed the entire wedding party.* A pleasant, tingling warmth spreads throughout his chest, indicating his master's amusement.

I too must remain innocent by appearances. The Lady and others who still blindly serve Kailon would surely raise a fuss. We can plan in peace if they remain ignorant of those plans.

Wearing a scowl to deter those wanting to chatter aimlessly, Jackson moves through the crowd. If he looks like he's on an important mission, people generally leave him alone.

You still have to make public amends with Marina.

The thought momentarily morphs Jackson's scowl into a sneer.

21

Quickly, he buries his distaste for the task.

She's been busy.

But she is currently alone and between tasks. Better yet, your mother is within sight. Go and make her happy by being a supportive brother.

He takes two steps in the appropriate direction before stopping.

What do I say to her?

Compliment her. Talk about the party. Ask for her forgiveness. What you say does not matter. Keeping the conversation civil is important. Do not let her spark an argument. Remember the goal. We must put her at ease. Get her to relax. If she is in the right state, I can examine the shield surrounding her mind. We must find out why she cannot be sensed from afar.

Aware the opportunity to speak with Marina could disappear any time, Jackson approaches and speeds them past the inane pleasantries before getting to his main point.

"Mother is eager for there to be peace between us," says Jackson. He leans close so the sound nullifying spell he'd placed around himself will guard the conversation from random eavesdroppers. "I am willing to forget the past, if you are."

At first, Marina's expression contains her usual contemptible calm, but his statement makes her stiffen. She stares hard at him.

"You can speak freely," he offers. "Nobody can hear what we say, but try to smile, for Mother's sake. Remember, you sought a truce first."

"That was more than three years ago, Jack," says Marina, tears shine in her eyes. She shifts to face away from the crowd of guests. "Before you poisoned our father!"

Keep her calm! Strong emotions interfere with my task.

"You'll never have proof, nor could you use it if you had it," says Jackson.

"I saw enough," Marina whispers. Her expression tells him she deeply regrets the knowledge. With effort, she projects an air of calm again. "I just want to know why him."

"Would you prefer it be you?" Jackson inquires.

His sister's expression answers affirmatively.

I can arrange that.

She surprises him by wrapping him in a tight hug, which he weathers by standing stiffly. Finally, Marina releases the embrace and grips Jackson's shoulders.

"What is it you truly want?" she asks. "It cannot only be money or power or affection. You could have all three if you helped Gabriel with his responsibilities and stopped actively pushing us away."

"I've not gone anywhere," says Jackson. "You're the one who fled your obligations."

Do not provoke her. I am close to answers.

Marina drops her hands from his shoulders but does not back away.

"You are right." Marina's gaze turns distant. "But I think I'm finally ready to change that."

What is she talking about?

I'll tell you later. Pretend to be pleased or at least don't scowl so hard.

The best Jackson can manage is a lesser frown.

It's not just power. It's ultimate power.

"You can't give me what I want," Jackson says truthfully.

"Nobody can," she replies sadly. "Only the One can give you peace."

He chuckles.

"What makes you think I need peace?" He surprises himself by really wanting to hear her answer.

"I can feel it in your spirit," Marina answers. "You feel … cold and dead."

Can she do that?

The Dark Man doesn't bother answering.

"I'm sure you have enough to worry about without adding my spiritual state to the mix," Jackson comments.

"You're my brother. I will always worry about you," says Marina. She stares into his eyes for a few seconds before glancing at the crowd. "I am glad you came to the wedding."

Concern is perfect. The shield source is close. Keep her in this state for a few moments longer.

"I still struggle to forgive you," Marina admits, "and I wish much was different between us. Can you forgive me?"

"For what?" Jackson's irritation spikes.

How does she always make everything about her?

"For leaving for so many years," says Marina. "It was selfish. I know that now. I thought only of my goals and dreams, not of what it would mean for the family. I missed so much time I could have spent with you or Gabriel. I left when he was a child, and now, he's a man."

"You can't control everything," Jackson says. "Why do you try?"

"It's not about control," Marina insists. She pauses, clearly trying to organize her thoughts. "It's about loving people. I left because I wanted to see the world beyond Caramore's barriers. The One gave us magical Gifts that can help people. We've been hiding them."

"The Arkonai care for the beggars well enough. Why concern yourself with their fate?" Jackson spares a second to wonder how his sister became so naïve. Neither of their parents ever displayed such foolishness.

I found the answer we seek. You can cease listening to her drivel.

"We were made to care for each other," says Marina. "My mistake was getting so wrapped up in my theories and studies that I neglected everything else, including our family. That is what I'm apologizing for."

"I accept," Jackson says with a gracious nod. "Thank you for sharing your thoughts. I will let you return to your duties."

Moving swiftly away from Marina, Jackson once again seeks a quiet place to think. His steps carry him into the gardens. Low-light magical lanterns illuminate the many winding paths. He hasn't been back here in years, but he recalls several isolated spots perfect for his current needs. The first option already holds a pair trying to avoid the general party, so he continues to the second choice near one of the smaller fountains. The location's far enough away from festivities that nobody bothered with a lantern, but Jackson doesn't mind. He finds the moonlight comforting.

"Who is it?" Jackson asks his master, once certain he is alone.

Gabriella. I suspected it might be her or Marcus, but I could not tell before tonight. You will have to deal with her first if you want to kill Marina.

"Do I have to kill her?" Jackson wonders. "Marina, I mean. What's the point? Our father's not around to change his will. She's won. I'll never inherit."

Absently, he conjures a coin and throws it into the fountain. A sudden, intense headache makes him stagger. It's gone an instant later, a sure sign it had no natural cause. Jackson recognizes his master's displeasure.

Forget the inheritance. You have enough money. You must kill Marina because she deserves it. She defied what is right by marrying an Arkonai man. They cannot be allowed to have a child.

"Could I not simply kill Daniel to prevent that?" Jackson asks. "I'm … not eager to cause my mother more pain right now."

She is a strong woman, your mother. Unclaimed, but we may yet save her from slavery to Kailon. This may be good for her. She clings to her children for strength. Not having them may force growth. Besides, she betrayed you.

Jackson conjures another coin and prepares to throw it, but his master's last statement grips his attention hard.

"What has she done?"

To make the idea of exerting her rights over the businesses more attractive to your sister, your mother changed the terms of succession. If Marina dies before having a child, her Arkonai husband will inherit what should be yours.

Heat burns within Jackson. He conjures a small fireball and casts it into the water where it sizzles, sputters, and dissipates. Marina would make her own will eventually. For all he knew, it might already be done. Succession had always been complicated. This wedding already almost guaranteed Jackson would never inherit the Castaloni lands and businesses. Though hard, he could accept losing them to respected Saroth, but being bumped even further down the list of candidates because of an Arkonai, was beyond insulting.

"She wouldn't," Jackson protests. Truthfully, he cannot predict much about his mother's feelings toward the Arkonai, but she never professed any great love for them either.

She did, but she can be forgiven. Everybody makes mistakes. She is desperate to save the businesses by forcing your sister's hand.

"How can I kill Daniel? He's a huntsman. Fighting is just about all they know."

He cannot be first. The problems must be dealt with in order. Gabriella protects Marina with a very thorough mental shield. She dies first.

"She's also just joined one of the most influential Saroth families," Jackson points out. "She'll be surrounded by servants and bodyguards. How will I get close enough to kill her, let alone get away with it?"

It may take years, but it can be done. Those servants you placed into the Polani household may eventually earn their fees. I will keep you apprised of developments. For now, you should hire competent assassins. I've prepared a list for you. We can discuss that later.

"How will we hide the murder from Marcus?"

Marina may have taken care of that for you.

Jackson flips the coin in his hand and catches it, waiting for his master to explain further.

At Marina's suggestion, Marcus and Daniel will soon be working together to show that Arkonai and Saroth can get along. They plan to have Gabriella help, but after a dangerous mission or two, they will insist she lend support from afar. We may be fortunate enough to have somebody kill them for us, but it's doubtful.

"Is Marina still staying in Temperance?" asks Jackson. "The mental shield won't matter if a normal spy can track her."

Concealment is only one benefit of such a shield. Her instincts will also be sharper. She currently resides in Temperance, but you must remove her from the city before approaching or any investigation will reveal your involvement. Once you have her, draw the huntsman into a trap and kill him.

Jackson experiences a sensation like a cloak being removed. His spirit feels lighter, and he understands his master has left him. Only then, does he let his thoughts wander.

Do I want to follow the orders?

The deal he struck with the Dark Man offered services in exchange for a crown. His master also helped him develop his skills as a Conjurer. At first, the aid Jackson rendered the Dark Man consisted mostly of arranging for bodies he could temporarily inhabit. They had moved on to him hosting the Dark Man's spirit for short periods of time.

What do I get that I don't already have?

His allowance affords him many luxuries and few responsibilities. He could claim more if he did more, but that would leave little time for helping his master return to Aeris proper. The land deserved a king. Why should it not be him? He could destroy the ineffective councils, purge the arrogant Arkonai, and rule the Bereft as he saw fit.

Gabriella. Marina. Daniel.

His master seemed adamant the three should die. At this point, Jackson doesn't care one way or the other. His previous campaigns against Marina had been more about securing the inheritance than entertaining genuine animosity for her as a person. Gabriella and Daniel would have zero significance to him if not for their involvement with

Marina.

What does he fear? The prophecy?

Jackson finds the idea ridiculous. He had never wasted much brainpower obsessing over dusty religious scrolls. Formal worship only matters to the weak who need saviors and redeemers and prophets for their pathetic lives to have meaning. Enlightened people only need their Gifts to succeed.

Tossing the coin into the fountain, Jackson watches the ripples and ponders the prophecy that concerns his master enough to seek death for Marina and Daniel. He'd heard numerous versions. About all they agreed upon was that a child of two races would use magic bracers to fight Darkland creatures and change the world.

Scholars—useless people to Jackson—argued about everything from what two races would bear this fabled child to what kind of change would come upon the world. Jackson's old master, August Polani, possessed at least three scrolls discussing the origins of the Lady's Chosen Redeemer. They couldn't even agree if the child would be descended of Saroth and Bereft, Bereft and Arkonai, or Saroth and Arkonai. While rare, the other two types of unions happened on occasion, but to Jackson's knowledge, Marina and Daniel were the first Saroth-Arkonai pair in centuries.

Real prophecy or not, my master has decreed you must die.

Chapter 4:
Far to Go

Heart and Hope Center, City of Temperance
One year after the marriage of Gabriella and Marcus
(Christa's twins are about two years old)
Pushing up the long sleeves of her green and blue dress, Marina settles onto the floor and reaches for the box of bandages. The young Conjurer tasked with summoning them from the factory in Outreach had dumped them in a heap after receiving them. Shaking her head, Marina plucks a partially unraveled roll off the top and rewraps it properly. She doesn't mind the work. In truth, she'd prefer to spend much more of her time doing mindless work instead of spending most days moderating disputes between house council members and arranging deals to improve things for one of the businesses.

You knew that would happen.

"Let me guess. Derrid was on duty today."

A female voice halts Marina's thoughts from wandering too far down a reflective path. As always, the light, charming Arkonai accent makes Marina miss her friend Christa.

Soon, Raelyn Cordova steps into view and sits across from Marina.

"He was distracted," Marina explains. "Babbled something about a courtship appointment tonight. If I made him stay and finish, we'd likely end up untangling as well as tightening the rolls." Setting the finished roll aside, Marina fishes out another and begins the simple but monotonous task again.

"A courtship appointment would be even more reason for me to stay and do a very thorough job," Raelyn says. Shaking out another bandage, she expertly fixes it and places it beside the one Marina laid to her left. "Never pass up a perfectly valid excuse, I say."

"Are your parents putting pressure on you again?" asks Marina, recalling the circumstances that brought the talented Healer to her doorstep.

"Father, no. Mother, yes," Raelyn says. She adds another two bandages to their growing stack. "I thought I'd escape some of that by moving hundreds of miles south, but I was mistaken. Now, Mother waxes long over how I should be more like the great and wonderful Ethan in written form. Does your mother compare you constantly to your brothers?"

"Not in the same way," Marina hedges, not ready to delve into a deep discussion of the stark differences between their cultures. "But I can assure you my mother had a lot to say about my marriage to Daniel, even if she said nothing directly to me about it."

"You're a legend among my peers," Raelyn declares. She finishes another roll and starts folding some larger sections of cloth used for more serious wounds. "A young woman who traveled the world, saved a village, and found forbidden love." She ends with a dramatic sigh.

The girl's summary of Marina's adventures prompts a smile. She quits her rolling work to stare at her companion, wondering how much of the story she should set straight. Telling the whole tale would take far longer than they have. After the current task, there are beds to make, linens to wash, supplies to inventory, books to balance, meals to deliver, and patients to visit.

"I had a lot of help with the village," Marina points out.

"Handsome help," Raelyn teases with an innocent look.

"Agreed." Marina laughs and thinks fondly of her husband. His warm brown eyes have long had the power to melt her heart. The mirth quickly fades, leaving a faint ache in her chest.

He's doing the One's work. Same as you. Just in a different place.

Wanting to think of something besides Daniel's long absences, Marina slides her mind over to the months in prison.

"There were less glamorous portions to the journey," Marina says. The One protected her in many ways and even blessed her with Daniel's presence throughout much of her term there. Still, the constant threat of physical harm and death had been difficult to bear.

"Father told me about the accident," says Raelyn tentatively.

"May I … see it?"

"There's not much left to see," says Marina. Nevertheless, she holds out her right arm at an angle that displays the vivid scar encircling her wrist. "The healing paste your father prepared worked well."

Dropping the cloth onto her lap, Raelyn gently takes Marina's hand.

"Your fingers are freezing," she notes. "Has it been like this ever since the incident?"

"I don't remember much about the early days," Marina admits. "I tried very hard not to feel anything, but I remember Master Cordova and Daniel hovering a lot."

"Sounds like something he would do," says Raelyn, running her fingers along the scar thoughtfully. "Would you like me to try to heal this?"

"Your father said healing could be dangerous since the wound was inflicted by magic," says Marina.

"I wasn't referring to Healing Gifts," says Raelyn, releasing Marina's hand. Her voice picks up pace and passion as she continues, "I've been experimenting with some herbs. Shermeece plus fialia with wild mint to make it palatable might work. Or something topical like arnought roots and westerval leaves. I don't think they'd interfere with each other, so we could try both if—"

Muffled shouts cut her off.

Marina and Raelyn scramble to their feet. Knowing a crash is inevitable, Marina reaches out to steady the younger woman. Once both have their balance, they exchange determined glances and dash out of the room. Mere seconds later, they exit the clinic's front door and take in a tense scene.

Their sudden arrival ends the shouting phase, but two groups of young men crowd the small courtyard. The group to her left consists of four Arkonai youths, while the one to the right has three Saroth. Both parties have at least one injured member. Marina quickly assesses the injuries. The Arkonai boy leans heavily on two companions. Large portions of his tan clothes bear burn marks, along with parts of the flesh along his arms, neck, and chin. The wounded Saroth boy sits on the ground, bleeding from multiple cuts. She cannot tell the full extent of his injuries because he's clutching his side, but his ability to sit up encourages her.

It's a disturbing, yet surprisingly familiar, scene.

"Raelyn, see to that one." Marina points to the Saroth boy. "Take him to Ward 2."

The young men bristle and open their mouths to protest, but Marina speaks first.

"If there's a chance any of those cuts contain toxins, she's far more qualified to treat him than I am," Marina explains. "If you don't want our help, there's the gate." She waves in the appropriate direction. "Otherwise, pick him up and follow my apprentice."

The collection of Arkonai observe these proceedings smugly, but once the Saroth disappear into the clinic with Raelyn, their collective attitude turns wary. Straightening, Marina clasps her hands serenely and addresses them.

"My name is Marina Castaloni-Saveron. Your presence here tells me you understand what we do. Our doors are open to everybody. There are separate sections, but I'm short of staff tonight. You're going to need to bring your friend into the same ward as the other young man."

"He did this!" The Arkonai youth standing slightly in front of his peers stabs a finger in his friend's direction.

"What does a Saroth know anyway?" mutters the boy supporting the burned man's right side. "Come on. Let's take him home. My cousin's a Healer. We can send for him."

"You're free to go." Marina's far too used to such statements to let them bother her. "But whatever you decide, do it quickly. Your friend doesn't have much time. If you're coming, follow me."

As expected, the Arkonai help their friend limp into the clinic.

Marina leads them through the main hallway down to Ward 2 and directs them to leave their friend on the bed placed next to the one holding the Saroth boy.

"What's wrong with these beds?"

Marina doesn't see the speaker, but she recognizes it as the young man who had wanted to leave.

"We are presented with two patients who require a lot of care this evening," Marina explains, moving to a supply cabinet to gather some clean bandages and a fresh batch of Master Cordova's healing cream. "If we're to provide the best care, we must be able to monitor both situations closely."

Next, she orders the healthy young men out except for the two she identified as acting leaders. The panicked, lost expressions from both groups tells her the normal leaders are her patients.

"Tell me your names," Marina instructs.

"Finley," says the Arkonai boy. He leans over his friend, who promptly passes out once settled upon the bed.

"Gio," says the Saroth boy.

"And who are we treating?" Marina asks. She continues peppering them with questions as she cleans and wraps the burns.

Over the next several minutes, the story unfolds. The dispute started with Erlo—the burned Arkonai boy—buying a fake Healing scroll from Jace—the boy with numerous cuts. When Erlo confronted Jace over the deception, Jace and his followers laughed. The fight quickly escalated from there. Erlo drew a dagger and slashed Jace several times. The Saroth boy retaliated with a small fireball.

"I never meant to hurt him." Jace voices the explanation in a shaky whisper. "I've done it dozens of times. Normally, the fireball singes the person's robes. That's all. Just a scare."

"Why was it different this time?" Marina glares at Jace, trying to keep her features neutral. She has a lot to say but knows there are more important issues to address first than the supreme stupidity displayed by both sides.

"The Healing scroll," Gio says miserably. "We added tazera powder to give it an impressive glow when somebody used it, so they'd think it worked."

Raelyn draws a sharp breath.

"You threw fire at tazera powder?" she asks. "You're lucky he still has limbs."

"He didn't have the scroll with him," Finley explains. "But he handled it when he read it for his mum."

"Will he live?" Gio asks.

"What do you care?" Finley's question holds considerable bitterness.

"We never—"

Marina stops Gio with a calming gesture so she can answer the question about Erlo.

"If there are no further complications, he should be fine in a few days," she reports, before directing the next question to Finley across Erlo's sick bed. "What's wrong with his mother?"

The young man shrugs.

"Not sure. They spent a lot on Healers early on, and she improved for a while." Finley looks sadly at his friend. "But the money ran out, and she declined. That was a few months ago. That's why he wanted the Healing scroll, even though I warned him against it."

"Do you know where they live?" Marina asks.

Finley nods slowly, looking distinctly uncomfortable.

"It's not far," he says. His right fingers tap nervously on the blanket near his friend.

"I see," Marina comments. She's no stranger to the attitude, though it does make her weary. She's not surprised to hear that they're close, for the clinic's central position had been chosen in the narrow, neutral band existing between poor sections housing Arkonai on the left and Saroth on the right.

We've made great gains, but we have far to go in healing the rifts.

"She won't come to the clinic because Lady Marina is Saroth," Raelyn says. Her tone conveys contempt.

"As you say," Finley admits, nodding at Raelyn.

"That is the stupidest thing I've—"

"Raelyn." At first, Marina calls the woman's name to interrupt her tirade, but a solution sails into her head. "Raelyn." Her second address is softer. "Are you done with Jace?"

"I fixed his side, but there's still some wrapping to do," Raelyn answers. Her fierce, conflicted expression says she's anticipating Marina's next question.

"Will you go with Finley to help this boy's mother?" Marina inquires.

"Does she deserve it?" Raelyn looks startled and disturbed by the question. "We've been here for years!" She shivers and replaces the irritation with projected calm. "I apologize." She directs the words to both Marina and Finley.

The boy stares at her, uncertain how to take her hostility and quick turnabout.

"If we waited for people to deserve our help, we'd be waiting a very long time," Marina notes. "Remember, you are treating more than a body. Besides, you cannot heal the unwilling. Offer your services and do your best to persuade this woman to accept aid. Don't fight her if she refuses you."

"I will try to help her," Raelyn promises, still not looking pleased with her assignment. "Should I finish here first?"

"Show Gio how to do it," instructs Marina. "If he wants to stay, he'll have to pitch in somehow."

Gio frowns but tentatively steps closer to Raelyn to watch as she wraps a bandage around a cut on Jace's left arm.

"Is there anything else I can do?" Finley asks tentatively.

"Not here," says Marina. "Your friend needs a lot of rest now.

I'll change the dressings in a few hours. Take Raelyn to Erlo's mother and return to me if she needs additional supplies for the work."

The young man accepts the instructions with a nod, squeezes his friend's shoulder, and jogs from the room with Raelyn close behind.

Chapter 5:
Demonstration

Main Council Chambers of the Tariku League, City of Dominance
Two years after the marriage of Gabriella and Marcus
(Christa's twins are about three years old)

The numerous mental pictures Gabriella and Marcus Polani shared with Daniel do little to capture the subtle beauty present within the Tariku League's formal meeting chamber. He compares the sight before him to the main chamber in Deliverance Hall, where the Arkonai High Council conducts serious business.

The design differs in several fundamental ways that reflect how the two magic races handle situations. Deliverance Hall boasts higher ceilings with many skylights. This chamber holds not one stitch of natural light. Instead, energy orbs of varying intensity surround the room, demonstrating how the Saroth people integrate magic into every aspect of their lives.

The Arkonai designers focused on a circular design with the council on one side and spectators in raised platforms off to the sides, mimicking an arena. Here, the nine Tariku League members sit on large, ornate chairs evenly spaced along a platform built well above the pit holding the plaintiffs and petitioners. The chair belonging to the Speaker is held even higher than the others.

Realizing he should be moving, Daniel quickens his pace as he walks past the dozens of rows containing benches for spectators. He follows Marcus down the slightly sloping floor to the right desk set out for people presenting cases to the council.

At first, the sheer size of the chamber surprises him, but further reflection convinces him the larger size fits. His people place great emphasis on a small number of people controlling the fate of many. While largely cut off from the wider world, Saroth invite members of all ages and social strata to take an interest in the Tariku League's public business.

Gabriella warned there would be a sizable crowd, but Daniel still finds it disconcerting to have so many eyes upon him. At one point in his life, he could hardly imagine meeting a Saroth. Now, he's surrounded by them.

Yet the one Saroth who matters is far from here.

Daniel spends the last few steps thinking of his wife. Marina's long dark hair may blend in with the crowd around, but she would quickly outshine any woman present. It's his brown locks that stand out as unusual. When they reach the desk, Gabriella shifts over to make room and smiles warmly in greeting. That would have struck him as odd without prior warning.

Direct contact with Minders is frowned upon during formal meetings, but Gabriella sends him a short burst of thought anyway.

Hush. You're thinking loudly.

Despite the presence of a chair and a bench, Daniel takes his cue from the others and remains standing. Below the platform holding the Tariku League members is a section for scribes and Minders. Destroyers and normal guards stand near entrances and at specific posts along the walls. Though Daniel doesn't sense them directly, Marcus warned that several Shapeshifters would watch proceedings in unobtrusive animal forms.

"Marcus Polani, you called for this meeting, so the floor is yours," says a woman seated on the central council chair. "Present your case."

Daniel doesn't react, but internally, he marvels at the idea of a woman rising to such a position of power. Thus far, few women have elected to join the hunting guild, let alone sought council seats.

Maybe things will change.

Since moving to Temperance and helping Marina with her clinic, he has met plenty of women capable of doing Seeker or Guardian work for the Guild.

A subtle mental nudge reminds him to focus on Marcus.

"Thank you, Speaker Amara. I seek permission to leave Caramore for an extended period of time," says Marcus. "As you know, Huntsman Seeker Daniel Saveron has spent the better part of the past two years helping me perform my investigative duties. It is well past time I return the favor."

"I have heard of the work you do," says Speaker Amara, "and I am curious as to the mechanics. Would you provide a brief demonstration?"

"What would you like us to do?" Marcus asks without hesitation.

"There are five silver coins around the room," says the Speaker. "Find them and project their locations for us. You may use several focusing crystals so everybody may see the Vision Cast."

Daniel bows to acknowledge the request. He and Marcus exchange grim nods. A test was inevitable. The exercise itself is a simple finding drill one would present to a first-year Seeker apprentice, but it's complicated by the lack of details concerning the type of coin and the many minds buzzing around them.

"You are welcome to move about as necessary," says the Speaker.

Marcus conveys their collective thanks while Daniel settles into the task. Moving out from behind the desk, Daniel paces in the open space in front of the council members. He needs to rein in his nerves in order to perform properly. He hasn't been this nervous since meeting Marina's father when they sought his blessing for their marriage.

You'll be fine. Marcus has an idea of the coins you're seeking. Relax and open your mind.

The encouragement comes from Gabriella, since Marcus is busy searching nearby minds for the information they seek. The Speaker likely didn't personally place the coins around the room. If she delegated the task, the responsibility probably passed to an assistant or apprentice.

After about a minute, Daniel sends a silent query to Gabriella about the delay.

The five coins went to different people to hide in places unknown to the others. He's checking for the last one now.

In a typical finding exercise, a similar coin would be provided to the Seeker. That would let him fully tap into his Gifts to follow the trail and get a sense for the object being sought.

He's got it. Your turn.

Images flow into Daniel. Five coins and five faces. A glance at the scribe's section reveals one of the faces. Bringing his Seeker Gifts to bear, Daniel follows the young man's recent history, essentially retracing his steps for the past few hours. When he reaches the point where the man stoops and places a coin under one of the benches, he relays the knowledge to Marcus by picturing the spot on a rough mental sketch of the room.

A collective murmur from the crowd draws Daniel's gaze upward. Marcus has positioned six focusing crystals above Daniel. The air between the crystals shimmers with magic as Marcus transfers the images from Daniel's mind onto the temporary screen. A scribe apprentice is dispatched to the location midway up the left side where he finds the first coin.

The process repeats as expected for three of the other coins, but when it comes to locating the last one, something feels wrong. There is a coin beneath one of the guard's boots, but it doesn't feel right.

It's too easy.

We could use easy right now. I'm not sure how much longer Marcus can last. He has a massive headache.

Show me the first image again. The coin handoff.

Gabriella pulls the memory transfer to the forefront of Daniel's thoughts. He watches it at normal speed then makes it repeat twice more at half speed.

She kept the last coin.

Once Daniel reaches his conclusion, he silently searches for the coin through his Seeker Gifts. A sense of it pulses from the Speaker's throne-like chair. It's sitting on the wide arm near her right hand.

Marcus shakes with fatigue but accepts the last image and dutifully provides an image for the crowd through a Vision Cast. He collapses onto the bench beside Gabriella as the picture fades.

The Speaker smiles and tosses the last coin down to the scribe apprentice who'd been collecting them as they were revealed. The boy races over to the desk where Marcus and Gabriella are sitting and carefully lays them out before them.

"That was quite impressive, but I see it's taken a toll on Master Polani," says Speaker Amara. "Let us adjourn for a half-hour before the final questions."

The crowd gets up and mills about, but Daniel moves behind the bench holding his friends. Gabriella has already sent a boy to fetch some water for Marcus. From this angle, Daniel gets a clear view of Gabriella's midsection.

"Are you both all right?" asks Daniel. He grips the back of the bench hard. "Is the baby safe?"

"That was harder than anticipated," Gabriella admits, "but we'll be fine." She flashes Daniel an amused grin. "And if you're this worried for me, I can't wait until Marina's expecting." She pats Daniel's hand. "For the record, women have successfully done this for centuries."

"But they've not taken on the level of mental strain you have," Marcus argues.

"I had a thought about that," Gabriella announces.

Both men look at her expectantly.

"If you want me to stay behind, then you have to compromise with me," she continues.

"Compromise how?" Marcus asks cautiously.

"Accept a substitute," Gabriella explains. "Today only proves you still need the support."

Marcus stares at his wife.

"You already have somebody in mind." His narrowed eyes hold a hint of accusation.

"I have somebody in mind," Gabriella confirms.

The exchange intrigues Daniel. He didn't think Minders could keep secrets from one another.

A tall woman appears at Daniel's side. She possesses the same dark hair as many Saroth, but her striking green eyes remind him of his friend Christa Lekros.

"Allow me to present Navina Christol," says Gabriella. "We've only met recently when I realized I couldn't go with you, but she's a powerful Minder and fast becoming a good friend."

"Lord Polani. Master Seeker. I am at your service," says Navina. "Lady Gabriella mentioned some travel would be involved, but I am not privy to the details."

"First rule if you join our little band: call me Daniel."

"The work we do is intense enough without any barriers between us," Marcus explains. "You have to trust us, and we have to trust you. That leaves little room for formalities."

They spend the rest of the short break chatting with Navina. Daniel can tell Marcus isn't thrilled with the idea of bringing a newcomer along, but they both know Gabriella is right. They will need help. He likes the Saroth woman well enough, but he's also worried about taking her beyond the magical barriers of Caramore. It's not like taking a traveler's portal to a neutral city. Their main goal will be tracking down dangerous men.

Adaram Serco will be traveling with you to protect her.

Before Daniel can thank Gabriella for the assurance, the Speaker officially instructs everybody to be seated again and resumes the meeting.

"You have shown that your Minder Gifts can be combined with Master Saveron's Seeker Gifts to good effect," says Speaker Amara. "But before giving you our blessing to take leave of your responsibilities, Master Polani, you must answer a few questions to our satisfaction." She waves for Marcus to approach.

He slowly rises, slips past Daniel, and stands before a bar that rose out of the floor while Daniel wasn't watching.

"First, is your house succession in order?" asks the Speaker.

"It is," Marcus answers. "I am acting head of my house. My father lives, but he is on a prolonged expedition into the Badlands. Should something happen to me, the Polani house council will appoint my wife, Gabriella, temporary head until our child comes of age."

"How old is your child?" asks the Speaker.

"He—or she—will arrive in a few days," Marcus answers.

"Unusual, but not unheard of," comments Speaker Amara. "It's also not enough. Who comes after your wife and child?"

"My sister, Janine, and my brother, Caleb," says Marcus. "After them, I have an uncle, Roberto, who has several children."

The Speaker turns to the Tariku League members to either side and receives several solemn nods.

"We are satisfied on that score," announces the Speaker. "Before we render a ruling, I would personally like to know what you expect to accomplish."

"We would like to right a wrong committed against the Arkonai Hunting Guild almost three years ago," Marcus explains.

"Three years?" The Speaker's surprise is clear in her tone. "What makes you think it can be righted after such a lengthy delay?"

"Daniel can testify that certain safeguards were taken," says Marcus. "He thinks they can last another two years or so, but an investigation could take us several months."

"I can see how that would benefit the Arkonai," says Speaker Amara. "But why is this important to you?"

"That is a longer tale." Marcus glances back at Daniel before finishing his answer for the Speaker. "Suffice to say a very special person taught both of us the value of building good will, especially between those granted Gifts by the One. If the whispers of coming dark times hold any truth, we will need allies."

Marcus's statements cause a stir, but the Speaker regains control quickly.

"Some may say your views are dangerously naïve, but you have our permission to pursue the ends described. You are dismissed."

Chapter 6:
Vassal

Lady Sierra's House of Discreet Transactions, City of Outreach
Same week (Two years after the marriage of Gabriella and Marcus)
(Christa's twins are about three years old)

Jackson Castaloni follows an attendant to a room midway down the first-floor hallway located behind the general meeting chamber. He never imagined stepping foot in a place like this, but he agrees that this phase of the plan should be kept away from official family business. After opening the door, the attendant steps aside and holds the door open for him.

"The other guest has already arrived," says the man. He holds a small scroll out to Jackson. "Your comfort and privacy are high priorities for us, but we also value your safety. If you need anything, simply activate this and a Minder will respond accordingly. Opening it should be enough to alert the staff something is amiss."

Accepting the panic scroll, Jackson steps into a small but tastefully decorated room. It features a couch, several large chairs, a tiny table, and two wooden chairs. A plain young man with black hair and dark eyes stands and bows politely.

Jackson stops two steps into the room. The door clicks shut behind him.

"I think there's been a mistake," he comments. There's no chance this young man is old enough to have built up the reputation of the assassin he's supposed to meet.

"No mistake, my lord," says the young man. "I am Federico. My

42

master sends his greetings and an apology for his caution. The authorities in Outreach have recently tripled the bounty on his head. He cannot safely conduct business in person."

"I was told I could meet Barsi today," Jackson says.

"And so you shall," says the youth. He waves to the table where a single wooden mug sits. "Allow me to explain my role as a vassal. Once I drink this, I will be directly connected to my master for a short time. When the effects wear off, I will fall unconscious and awaken in a few hours with no memory of what has transpired between you."

Jackson stares at the young man, trying to measure his sincerity. *Does he speak truth, Master?*

It's a very difficult potion to master. Expensive and dangerous for the user too. But such things do exist.

"Why would you take such a risk?" Jackson wonders.

"The money," answers the young man. Picking up the mug, the youth salutes Jackson with it and drinks the liquid inside. The change happens quickly. The man's features harden. His posture straightens.

"Be seated. Our time is short." The voice coming from the young man is distinctly different from the one before. "I am Barsi. My people tell me you have a job offer. I usually only consider straight contract kills, but the amount spoken of has made me curious. What is it you desire?"

"I need a building destroyed," says Jackson, sinking onto the free wooden chair. "In Temperance."

"A neutral city?" Barsi's inflection carries his surprise, but the emotion also shows up on the vassal's features. "That's going to cost extra."

"Can you do it?" Jackson asks flatly.

"I can do anything," answers Barsi. "Convince me it's worth my time. Which building do you need destroyed and what is your motive for having it destroyed? What level of destruction do you need?"

"Why do you care?" Jackson asks.

"People don't last long in my line of work by taking any contract that comes their way," answers Barsi. "The building's size, warding status, purpose, number and type of occupants, and so forth, will affect how many incendiary scrolls must be employed and the damage rates they need to achieve to be effective. If you need the structure reduced to ashes, that's a far different job than burning the interior."

"It's a healing clinic run by a Saroth woman who married an Arkonai," Jackson answers. "I need the occupant and her husband to quit the city altogether."

"Any gang of thugs could read a destructive scroll," Barsi notes. "You could make it more impressive by seeding the place with tazera powder or something with similar properties. Why come to me?"

"The woman who runs the clinic doesn't scare easily," says Jackson. "This may be a prolonged campaign. I'm told you have the right connections. I need her driven out of Temperance."

"A kill order would be easier," says Barsi.

"Cheaper too, but that's not the job." Jackson sincerely wishes it was the job. His master's elaborate schemes don't always make sense to him. Every few months it seems the Dark Man changes his mind about Marina.

There must be something more to wanting her alive for now.

There is, but we will discuss that later.

"She's under the protection of a Huntsman Seeker," Jackson continues.

The current plan involves removing Daniel and Marina from Temperance, dealing with Gabriella, isolating Marina, and then dealing with her.

"Their powers are limited," says Barsi. "The Seeker would need a direct contract with her to be able to intervene every time there's danger, but I will keep that in mind as I plan."

"Do you accept the job?" Jackson asks, needing solid confirmation one way or the other. He has a few more options should Barsi refuse.

"Yes. I believe it will be interesting," says Barsi. "Did you have a specific timeframe in mind?"

"Soon," answers Jackson. "I have other plans to place, but I'd like this detail completed first."

"Do you need any referrals?" inquires Barsi. "I can recommend Shapeshifters, Conjurers, Destroyers, Minders, Healers, and even a Guardian or two. It doesn't cost you extra as the referral payment comes from them. As you can see, I also have a skilled potions master at my disposal."

"We can discuss future arrangements after this assignment," says Jackson.

"As you wish," says Barsi. "If you have any last details I need, give them now. The potion is all but spent."

"The target is Marina Castaloni-Saveron," says Jackson.

"I know. There is only one Saroth-Arkonai pair in Temperance.

I will find her," explains Barsi.

"I need her out of the city but alive," Jackson clarifies. "That's very important."

"It will be as you say," Barsi promises. "Kill the boy and leave half my fee with the body. I will require the second half once the job is completed. Feel free to stay in the room. It's reserved for the next several hours. Federico won't bother you. Move him to the couch once he's dead if you want him out of the way."

Once finished speaking, the young man's eye close and he slumps forward onto the table, knocking the mug to the floor.

"Why are we playing games with them?" Jackson asks.

Best follow our friend's instructions. I will be able to converse more easily though a fresh body anyway.

Drawing a dagger, Jackson quickly follows the order. His face scrunches with distaste as blood gets on his hand. Conjuring some water and a fresh cloth from the Veil, Jackson carefully cleans the dagger and his hands.

"I hate killing," says Jackson. He frowns at the body. "Why do you make me do it?"

"Because you need the practice." This time, the deep, unhurried voice that comes from Federico contains far more confidence and an air of ancient wisdom. The body sits up and stares at Jackson with empty white orbs instead of eyes. "The tasks I have for you will be difficult. Your heart must have the proper calluses around it. Think of it as an exercise, akin to your rigorous Conjuring studies."

"We're back to not killing my sister right away," Jackson says, tucking his dagger into a pocket and turning away from the animated corpse. Seeing only the whites of the eyes always disturbs him. "Why?"

"Daniel Saveron has become quite the Seeker in the last few years," says the Dark Man. "The Arkonai High Council may promote him to huntmaster status soon."

"Good for him, but why should I care about his good fortune?"

"You don't have to care," responds the Dark Man, "but I require his services."

"You want to capture Marina to force his compliance?" Jackson's inflection renders the words as a question.

The body shakes its head vigorously.

"Such crude plans nearly always fail," says the Dark Man. "No. For the job I have in mind for Daniel, I need him completely committed."

Jackson sits on the couch and conjures a glass of ice water.

"I doubt he would support our cause," notes Jackson. "He seems committed to the One and the Lady of Light."

The Dark Man twists Federico's features into a fine sneer.

"Do not mention them!" He spits the words with disdain.

"My apologies, Master," Jackson says quickly. "But the point remains, the man isn't likely to do us any favors."

"He will if he thinks it's the only way to save his dear wife."

"How shall we convince him of that?" Jackson plants his feet more firmly and leans forward, eager to hear the answer.

"We turn Marina into one of the true undead."

True undead? Like Denkari?

"Similar, but very different," answers the Dark Man. "The Denkari are spirit warriors who helped me fight the Charlatan. True undead wander mortal planes until released by those who create them."

The Dark Man's words strike Jackson hard. He half-listens as his master elaborates on the new plan.

"I see this is too much for you right now," says the Dark Man, sensing Jackson's distraction. "I have other servants to check with. Return to your studies at Fort Medron. Search your heart. If you cannot do what must be done, I will release you from our agreement."

Jackson recognizes his master's words as a threat, but the ice chilling his heart stems from the idea of turning Marina. He's been at odds with her for over a decade. Killing her strikes him as a sad but inevitable next step. From a certain viewpoint, he can even attempt to frame it as a kindness to her. The move will hurt their mother, but she'll still have him and Gabriel to comfort her. Forcing Marina to become undead is much worse.

Can it be done?

He doesn't realize he's seeking an answer from his master until receiving only complete silence for several seconds.

Over the years, Jackson's summoning skills have improved much. He can call Darkland spirits into certain bodies and inanimate objects, but he has never tried to go the other way, though he's read quite a bit about the theory.

Most people never draw a distinction between zombies and undead, instead choosing to use the terms interchangeably. But Jackson knows better. A normal zombie can be created by casting a soul out of a body and reanimating the remains or calling forth a wandering soul to temporarily inhabit old bones. Making an undead capable of following

46

orders involves imprisoning a soul yet keeping it close to the body or calling forth a dark spirit to command it. The academic question of *how* intrigues him, but the idea of condemning his sister to such a fate disturbs him.

Does she really deserve to become a soul slave?

Jackson has little doubt Marina would gladly die for many reasons. Becoming an unwilling servant of his master would be a fate much worse than death. At least death would release her to whatever world lies beyond this one.

Can I do that to her?

His gaze falls upon the young man's body. The head leans back, and the eyes stare up at the ceiling, having reached that position when the Dark Man vacated the body. A short period of introspection digs up a faint sense of regret and remorse, but the feelings don't cause Jackson any real pain. His mind travels back to Aridel where his master first bid him to kill somebody. He hadn't been able to follow through and threw up afterwards anyway.

I've come far. Maybe by the time I gain the skill, I will have the desire to use it.

Chapter 7:
Fire is Fire

Heart and Hope Center, City of Temperance
Almost a month after Katrina's birth
(Christa's twins are still three years old)

"Who would do such a thing?" cries a Bereft woman.

"Stay back!" calls a man. Anger gives his words a crackling energy that rivals the scene unfolding behind him. "There's magic involved!"

Whole body shaking, Marina sinks to her knees and gazes up at the building she's poured her heart and soul into for over four years. Fire engulfs the entire structure. An echo of the fire warms her chest. Reaching out with her spirit, she tries to tamp down the energy, but the fire flares, reinforcing the man's words.

"Help!"

The familiar female voice followed by a series of coughs cuts to Marina's core.

Raelyn!

Springing to her feet, Marina charges forward two steps before somebody yanks her to a stop.

"You'll never make it." This time, the man's tone holds only resignation. "One more explosion and the whole thing could collapse."

"I have to help her!" Marina declares.

Help who? What's going on?

Instead of explaining the situation to Gabriella, Marina allows the Minder to freely search her recent memories. She had only been a few blocks away when the trouble burst into fiery life. Since the clinic

48

resided in a dense section of the city, a crowd sprang up instantly.

Raelyn's inside.

We can save her.

How?

Reach out to the fire. You've done it before in Aridel.

That was a small bonfire started by the wind. This is—

No different in principle.

There's magic involved.

Fire is fire. We are Saroth. The One has gifted many of us with a degree of control over the element. It won't be easy, but we can save her if you are willing.

Tell me what to do.

Reach out with your spirit. Find the fire. Smother it. You know how to create fire. Follow the process in reverse. If you can't do that, completely open your mind to mine. I may be able to lend you one of my Gifts.

Marina knew little about Minder specialties, but over time, she's come to appreciate the differences between Gabriella's Gifts and Marcus's. Her adopted sister excelled at mental shields but also possessed the ability to move objects and temporarily work through others. Marcus could move objects around him and Vision Cast but transfer of any sort was beyond him.

Letting her shoulders relax, Marina steps out of the man's grip and closes her eyes. Upon reaching out with her spirit, she senses four spots that are distinctly hotter than the others. Concentrating on the one nearest Raelyn, Marina finds the magical source and seizes hold of it. A burning sensation engulfs her chest.

Let me help.

Marina has no energy to think a reply, but she drops down to her hands and knees and mentally reaches for Gabriella. A sharp pain pierces her head, but she ignores the discomfort and reaches for the fire again. This time, she grips the source and tugs it toward herself. An enchanted scroll flies out of an open window and zips toward Marina. Once it's clear of the building, she mentally launches it skyward as she did with the fireball in Aridel.

Three to go. You can do this.

Spots float before Marina's vision. Her head feels like it hosts multiple spikes. A new sharp pain has started in her side. Connecting their minds this closely automatically means Gabriella will feel everything Marina does.

You're in pain too.

Doesn't matter. Work's not done.

Murmurs of awe and fear rise up from the crowd around her, but Marina ignores them. Locating the second and third fire sources, she repeats the process in rapid succession, yanking the scrolls clear of the building and flinging them up into the night air before releasing them.

"Stop this," hisses a male voice. "You'll kill yourself."

Strong hands pull Marina up to her feet. Exhausted, she starts to collapse, but he steps close enough to brace her back with his chest. His arms loop around her waist, and his head hovers near hers. Even with energy orbs casting light on the courtyard, nobody sees the tiny dagger the man presses hard against her left side. A casual viewer would think them lovers mourning a collective loss.

Sweat and tears mingle on Marina's face. She can't even muster the energy to be alarmed by the man's proximity, though the menacing voice quality and the dagger's presence finally register.

"Be still and listen," says the man.

The fog of shock blasts away as Gabriella asserts her Gifts on Marina's mind.

Clarity returns.

"You … did this." Marina watches smoke billow out of several windows. She's pleased to see less flames, but the battle to salvage the situation is far from over. "Why?"

Her question goes unanswered.

"You will let the building burn and leave the city, or I will kill the girl myself." The man speaks the threat directly into Marina's right ear, but with the crowd this agitated, he could shout and be ignored.

"Save her," Marina orders.

"Why should I?" asks the man.

"Because if you won't, I will," Marina declares. "Whatever the consequences."

"Swear an oath upon the girl's life to leave Temperance and never return, and it will be done," says the man.

Do not swear anything.

"You have my word," Marina promises, ignoring Gabriella. The taste of smoke and ash upon her tongue turns the words bitter.

"Her life will always rest upon your words," warns the man. "I will watch from afar. You have an hour to be outside the city limits." He adjusts his grip and makes Marina repeat the vow aloud.

As the last word passes her lips, the man shoves her to the

ground and disappears into the milling crowd. Small stones dig into her hands, but she barely registers the new discomfort. Getting to her knees, Marina looks around cautiously, but as she never saw the man, she has no hope of identifying him.

He is gone.

Can you track him?

Yes, but you're in no condition for a chase. Besides, what would you do if you could follow him?

Before she can work up a decent answer for her sister, somebody slams into Marina, undoing her efforts to rise.

Raelyn clings to her with desperate strength and sobs in her arms. The young woman's clothes and hair reek of more smoke, but this time, Marina finds the scent comforting. She even welcomes the ache in her back caused by the involuntary shudders of sobs.

With the excitement over, the crowd soon disperses, leaving the two women alone in the empty courtyard. The energy orbs still lend enough light to see by. Somewhere inside the structure, a crack sounds as more of the building crumbles.

Marina tries to wrench her attention away, but part of her needs to bear witness to the clinic's final moments.

You should move. There's still danger if the building collapses.

Help me.

Marina, you're in no condition—

It will need to be rebuilt anyway. We can't let the destruction spread further.

Gabriella reluctantly agrees, and together, they reach out and place pressure upon the weak points, allowing the floors and walls to fall inward.

The effort makes Marina dizzy. Her breaths turn ragged. She can't even cry, but her apprentice sheds enough tears for both of them.

When Raelyn's sobs fade to sniffles, Marina pulls back far enough to examine the woman. Raelyn's hands look fine, but her wrists bear the telltale marks of rough rope bindings. Marina looks closer.

"I had to heal them," Raelyn says, sounding almost embarrassed. She swipes a dirty hand across her face to clear it of tears, leaving a wide, sooty smudge across her left cheek.

"What happened after I left?" Marina uses a clean section of robe to dab at the tear streaks and dirt on Raelyn's face.

"I gave our last patient some healing paste and sent him on his way. Then, I restocked the cabinets in Ward 3. As I went to leave, something struck me from behind." Raelyn touches a spot on the right side of her head. "Here." She draws a shaky breath but forges on with her story. "When I awoke, fire was everywhere. It burned my hands and the ropes. I remember healing my hands and then collapsing by the window." Fresh tears pool in her eyes. "This was no accident. Why would anybody burn down a place of healing?"

"It was a threat," Marina answers. Suddenly aware of the passage of time, she climbs to her feet and helps Raelyn up as well. "A very effective threat."

"A threat from whom?" Raelyn wonders. "Against whom? To what end?"

"I'm leaving," Marina says.

"To go where?" Raelyn asks.

"Out of Temperance," Marina replies. Unshed tears sting her eyes.

"I don't understand," says Raelyn, catching Marina's arm. "It's just a building. We can fix this."

Heart crumbling, Marina draws the younger woman into another hug.

"The threat wasn't to the building. It was to the people. It was to you." She launches into a short version of her experience.

Breaking free of the embrace, Raelyn stands stiffly. Her expression darkens with anger.

"I don't care what anybody says," she declares. "We should fight this."

"With what?" Marina inquires.

"Guards. Huntsman. Those Nokarti Assassins you've talked about," says Raelyn. "I don't know, but you have to stay. Think of the good we've done, the good we have yet to do!"

"Not if it risks your life. All the man wanted was a promise for me to leave Temperance," Marina explains. "No place, no ambition is worth a person's life. I will gladly go."

"Go where?" Raelyn's second iteration of the question contains both her frustration and her disbelief. "This is your home! What about your husband?"

"I have called many places home," says Marina, forcing a sad smile. "And my husband is a Seeker. He'll be able to find me."

"Can I go with you?" Raelyn wonders. "You can teach me more about finding things with healing properties out in nature instead of buying them at a market."

Marina studies her apprentice's face while considering the request, detecting both eagerness and fear. For a moment, she imagines taking Raelyn. Travel with a companion is always easier, but it also means more responsibility. An uneasy feeling crawls through her gut at the thought of the man targeting Raelyn. Marina fervently wants to believe leaving will end matters with the mysterious man, but she's not that naïve.

Why does it matter where I live?

We can discuss that shortly but give the girl your answer.

A course of action crystalizes in her mind.

At last, Marina shakes her head.

Raelyn's head bows in defeat.

Reaching out, Marina tips her chin up so their eyes meet again.

"Stay here and rebuild the clinic," Marina instructs. "I will make sure you have the proper funds to restore and expand, but the details are in your hands. This is important. *You* and this place are important for changing hearts and minds."

"How will I know what to do?" Raelyn sounds truly lost.

"Speak with the One," Marina answers. Her sad smile spreads. "Invite your father down from Aridel. I'm sure he'll have some opinions to share."

The suggestion earns an amused sniff from Raelyn.

"Opinions are one thing he's never short of," she says. "Will I see you again?"

"It's probably safer for you if you don't," Marina says honestly, "but I will be in touch when I can."

Bracing her heart for new pain, Marina turns away and dashes home to pack for the road. She doesn't know how much time has passed, but she senses the man's deadline closing in.

Where should I go?

Take a traveler's portal to Outreach. There's an office you can stay in tonight and regroup.

Many years of mental contact lets Marina feel Gabriella's hesitation.

What's wrong?

The timing is terrible, but I need to ask you for a big favor.

Chapter 8:
Delivery Duties

Polani Estate, City of Jorash
Same day
(Christa's twins are still three years old)

Daniel follows the servant through many corridors. He hasn't really spent time in a private residence this large since visiting Christa's childhood home ages ago. He knew Marcus came from a prominent and wealthy family but walking down hallways whose carpets likely cost more than some villages adds a new perspective.

He seems so normal.

Good morning, Daniel. Thank you for coming. I apologize for not meeting you in person. I know our customs seem strange to you, and you'd rather be with Marina. We can speak through the door when you get here. How is she?

Shaken but stubborn. Said I couldn't step foot in the house she rented for us until I delivered these Teleportation scrolls to you personally.

He receives an amused sense from Gabriella.

I'm sorry the delivery duties fell to you. We don't have to speak if you need to leave right away. I know getting here was a journey.

Daniel grunts, recalling that journey. Alerted by Marcus to the clinic's destruction, he had followed his wife's trail from Temperance to Outreach where he found her at the Castaloni shipping offices. She'd barely kissed him before shoving two scrolls into his hands and sending him out the door with instructions to personally deliver them to Gabriella. Marcus had tried to come but agreed to stay with Marina since

54

being near, yet unable to see, Gabriella and his newborn daughter would have been maddening. The second phase to his journey had taken Daniel from Outreach to Dominance where he waited almost half an hour before the Tariku League granted him permission to travel from there to Jorash, as long as he accepted an armed escort.

If I return to my wife and your husband without checking on you properly, how do you think they're going to react?

I concede the point, and I welcome the company. Isolation can be difficult, even with a beautiful baby to love.

When the servant stops, Daniel does as well. His two escorts also stop.

The servant knocks gently.

"Huntsman Seeker Daniel Saveron has arrived," he announces. "Would you like me to stay, my lady?"

"No, thank you, Rivan." Gabriella's voice comes through the door perfectly clear. "Please ask the escorts to move to the end of the hall. I would like to speak with the huntsman privately."

"Right away." The servant frowns but motions for the escorts to retreat.

"Wait one moment while I activate the privacy scroll," says Gabriella.

You need a privacy scroll in your own home? Daniel eyes the sturdy door separating him from his friend. *And how does Marcus stay away?*

Think of the isolation month as an extension of pregnancy. He's never seen our daughter in person, so the anticipation can build. Though between you and me and the privacy spell, he's felt her mind already and he's thoroughly smitten. Would you like to sense her? Transferred images are always more powerful when close. I'm sure Marcus would appreciate the gesture.

Stretching forth with his Seeker Gifts, Daniel senses two presences near the door. One gives him the impression of weariness while the other projects serenity. He also detects a third presence further back in the room. Alarm spikes through Gabriella, mentally striking Daniel as well. The surprise causes him to withdraw his spirit from the room, but he doesn't react externally. His entire being fills with the peaceful sensation projecting from the sleeping child.

"I'm sorry, Daniel," Gabriella whispers, releasing the hold on his spirit. "I should have known better."

"I don't understand," he admits.

"The privacy spell will keep our conversation completely

confidential if needed," Gabriella explains, "but I never meant for you to have to bear this knowledge."

"Two spirits," he murmurs, searching his feelings for confirmation.

"We're not safe," says Gabriella, speaking softly despite the privacy spell.

"Come with me to Outreach," Daniel suggests. "Whatever your fears, we can fix them. I can find huntsmen to watch over you day and night."

"That would only make things worse." Gabriella's words pick up speed as she tries to conquer the cultural divide in one short speech. "Our enemies would view such a move as a challenge, and support for them would grow."

"If you know your enemies, we can fight them," Daniel insists.

Gabriella laughs bitterly.

"I wish that were true, but Saroth do not handle problems and rivalries like your people do," Gabriella explains. "We hire assassins."

"Did something happen?" Daniel demands.

"Not directly." Gabriella sounds frustrated by her inability to explain things adequately to him. "But our child changes everything."

Children.

Please, Daniel, even in your thoughts be cautious. House wards are never completely impenetrable.

"Every heir elevates a house's status," Gabriella explains without missing a beat. "That will anger rivals. Twins are seen as a blessing from the One and would give the Polani name much more influence within the Tariku League. We don't have a voting member on the council, but we have many advocates to raise our concerns. News of twins would stir up trouble, and I don't even believe those rivalries are the most serious threats. Marcus collects more political enemies by doing his job at the Academy of Arts and Sciences."

What does he do?

Put bluntly, he's a spy. That's why it took so long for him to receive permission to work with you. They feared he would betray them some way.

"What can I do to help?" Daniel asks, wrestling with a feeling of helplessness.

"Hide my son."

Gabriella's answer stuns Daniel on multiple levels. Her pained tone tells him the request goes much deeper than tucking the child away for a few months. It means keeping his existence a secret from everybody, including Marcus. Anger flares within him. Marcus deserves the chance to know both of his children.

"I know you're angry Marcus can never know." Gabriella's voice cracks with grief.

"Why the boy?" Daniel demands, hating himself for hurting his friend this way. "How'd you make that decision?"

You're practically daring your enemies to target your daughter. He knows the final statement's unfair, but he can't stop the thought from forming.

"I had no choice!" She sounds very close to tears. "Somehow, Katrina reached out to her father long before her birth. Marcus touched her thoughts before I did. I only barely had time to shield Adam's thoughts from him."

"You planned this for a while," Daniel notes, trying to keep his tone neutral so their verbal wounds can heal a moment. "Why involve Marina and me?"

The tactic works. Gabriella sounds calmer as she answers him.

"If you agree to help, I need you to make this an official contract to further guarantee your silence. Then, I need you to enter the room and collect Adam. Use the Teleportation scrolls Marina gave you to take him to some friends who recently lost a child. They already know to expect him."

"Is that allowed within the terms of your isolation?" Daniel asks tentatively. "Won't my escorts protest?"

"I will deal with them," says Gabriella. "You'll be far away before they can intervene, but do not teleport directly out of Caramore. Go back to Dominance and take the traveler's portal wherever you need to go. The magical barrier is meant to keep people out, but it works both ways. Tell the guards you're under contract with me, and they will let you through."

"Are you sure you want to do this?" Daniel asks, silently pleading with his friend to see reason. "I can stop working with Marcus. You'd probably have fewer enemies to deal with when not associated with the dreaded Arkonai."

His attempt to lighten the mood fails.

"No." Gabriella's answer is surprisingly firm. "I will tell Marcus in time, but right now, Adam's safety is more important. My friends are good people. They will love him well." She sounds like she's trying to convince herself.

"Tell Marcus," Daniel begs. "He deserves to be involved in this decision."

"My husband is a very powerful Minder, but he has no ability to hide most thoughts," says Gabriella. "If he knew, word would spread, and our enemies would find our son."

"You don't know that!" Daniel argues. "You can't know that."

"I can't explain the knowledge," says Gabriella. "It's mostly a feeling, and I'm explaining this poorly."

"Convince me." Daniel glares at the door as he levels the challenge.

"I love Marcus." Gabriella lets the declaration linger a few beats before continuing. "The One knows I don't want to hurt him."

"What about hurting yourself?" Daniel asks. "Sending your son away is going to kill a part of you. I hear that much in your voice."

"I'm terrified," Gabriella freely admits. "But not in the way you think." She draws and releases two breaths before speaking again. "I'm not afraid of standing by Marcus or helping with his work. I accepted those risks long ago when I fell in love with him."

"Then what's the problem?" Daniel wonders. "He had enemies before. He has enemies now. What's the difference?"

"There's a darkness growing in the world." Gabriella's words are barely audible. "When I look at my children, I see they're special. It's more than the love any new parent experiences. It's a pure knowledge that they're meant to heal the world's brokenness. That makes the Outcast their enemy. I will do anything and everything to keep his attention off them, including part with them."

Soft sobs reach Daniel through the door. He waits out a very awkward minute before speaking.

"Let me in then. I will take him where you wish," Daniel promises.

"Set up the contract," says Gabriella.

Daniel does so. Opening a space in the Veil beyond the door, he pulls out a pre-written basic contract, closes his eyes, and makes the proper adjustments. Next, he retrieves an ink jar and a quill for Gabriella to sign the contract.

"Finished," she calls.

Let me get him ready for you.

Letting the contract return to the Veil, Daniel calls out a Teleportation scroll, readies it for reading, repairs the small tear, and waits. The movements are slightly clumsier than usual due to the door in between, but he manages fine.

The door is unlocked. You may enter.

Swinging the door open, Daniel slips inside.

The escorts shout, but the sound gets muffled as Gabriella slams the door and locks it again.

"Thank you." Gabriella swiftly places a small bundle in Daniel's arms. "I've filled in your destination. Take Adam and go. Give Marcus and Marina my love."

Daniel's not happy about the contract, but he can't refuse either. He wants to comfort Gabriella, but she looks like any sympathy will shatter her composure. For his part, Adam sleeps peacefully. His dark hair is fuzzy and soft. His olive skin tone reflects his mother more than his father. Tucking the infant against his side, Daniel reads the spell off the scroll.

Gabriella's room vanishes, and Daniel finds himself in a field next to a tiny cabin. A woman pacing in front of the door freezes and stares at him.

"Aldo! He's here!" cries the woman. She rushes toward Daniel for several paces before halting and gripping her dress nervously. "Is Lady Gabriella well?"

"As well as she can be," Daniel replies, still cradling the child against his side.

A man rounds the side of the house and rushes to the woman.

"Is that him?" The woman's question sounds hopeful and breathless. "He's so small."

Daniel studies them. Their clothes look careworn and much repaired. They wear guarded expressions, but there's also compassion in them.

Deciding to trust Gabriella's instincts, Daniel places the baby into the woman's arms then pulls out the second Teleportation scroll. Before he can activate it and travel to Dominance, the woman hits him with two more questions.

"Is she right? Is he in danger?" The woman clutches the infant tightly.

"Are we in danger?" asks the man, stepping closer to his wife.

"You should be safe," Daniel assures them. "We three and the boy's mother are the only souls who know his true identity, and I can guarantee she will work very hard to keep him safe from afar."

With nothing else to say, Daniel teleports to Dominance, then finds the portal to Outreach. Even if he cannot share the truth with Marcus and Marina, he's eager to see them.

Chapter 9:
Wanderer's Heart

Courtyard Ruins, Fort Merit
Two and a half years after the marriage of Gabriella and Marcus
(Christa's twins are about three and a half years old)

Where is he?

To amuse himself, Jackson counts the paces needed to cover the courtyard's length. It doesn't work well because his distracted state has him changing directions often. Small trees and large, moss-covered rocks block any direct route he could take anyway. The Arkonai stopped maintaining most forts a few centuries ago, giving the land much time to reclaim the space. That any ruins remain speaks of lingering magic.

You have as much of a wanderer's heart as your sister.

Jackson grunts at this revelation, but he does not deny it. Over the years, he has come to think of the various fort remains as personal getaways, though he's only spent significant time at the one he semi-restored.

As for Barsi, he's not pleased by your summons, so he's making you wait. He is also be preparing a trap for you, hence our current arrangement.

The Dark Man's explanation does not make the wait any easier to bear, but Jackson's grateful for it all the same. Their current arrangement involves the Dark Man temporarily indwelling Jackson. He's never enjoyed hosting the dark spirit, but he accepts it as a necessary evil.

He failed. Marina's still out of reach.

We need to be more specific with the contract next time,

and I think we're overthinking this.

Before Jackson can inquire further, a faint popping sound alerts him to a Teleportation scroll being activated. He shuffles back two steps to give the person room to appear. Under the Dark Man's control, he retreats three additional steps.

Seven men appear. Each man touches the shoulder or the arm of the one next to him, allowing them to travel with the one who controls the Teleportation scroll.

Jackson conjures a small dagger but keeps his arms down at his sides.

A tense moment ensues.

The men quickly fan out, three moving left and three moving right of their leader. The two closest to Barsi must be Destroyers, for they create bolts of lightning and hold them like swords. One vanishes into the air in a bird form too swiftly for Jackson to identify. Another two conjure long wooden staffs. The last man simply retreats a few steps.

Jackson watches the posturing with contempt.

"I thought we had a private meeting," he comments, tucking his dagger into a pocket inside his robes.

"We do," says Barsi. "One of my companions will make certain it stays private. My apologies for startling you, but I would like these negotiations to proceed favorably."

"As would I," Jackson says, letting a feral grin form. A thrill courses through his entire being. He recognizes it as the Dark Man's influence, but for once, it doesn't terrify him. "Allow me to clarify that you should hope we reach favorable terms. I would like to offer you a contract."

"What do you need done this time?" asks Barsi. "And once again, why should I care?"

Play upon his hatred for the titled houses.

"You can strike a powerful blow to your enemies," says Jackson.

"Which house?" Barsi asks. A frown shows his desire to appear disinterested, but a shift in his stance says otherwise.

"Polani," Jackson answers.

Barsi's shoulders relax.

"They're not at the top of my list of deserving houses, but you may continue," says Barsi. "How shall I strike this powerful blow you speak of?"

"Kill Gabriella," Jackson answers.

A brief silence falls.

"My companion says the current matron of House Polani is called Elena." Barsi tilts his head curiously. "This Gabriella may not gain the title for many years. Why do you wish her dead?"

"Why do you care?" Jackson retorts. "Your reputation speaks of discretion."

Barsi grips his head. The Minder with him must be flooding him with information.

"I'm told the lady had a child recently. She's in isolation. Even when that ends, I doubt she'll leave the main estate for some time," Barsi explains. "Infiltrating such a place could take many months, possibly years. You don't have the funds to hire me for that long."

"I have access to something you want," Jackson offers. "Four Teleportation scrolls, and another two upon completion."

"I'm glad you said something," says Barsi.

At his gesture, the men with him spread out further, creating a semi-circle around Jackson.

The connection to the Dark Man lets Jackson sense the Shapeshifter taking a position behind him.

"I imagine your sister would pay several more than that for your return," Barsi continues.

Jackson silently congratulates his mother and Mika Forester for a stellar public relations campaign. At the same time, his confidence in Barsi's vaunted reputation for information wanes.

She would pay but not solely to save you. I am surprised nobody has bled the Castaloni holdings thus before now.

The managers still conduct most transactions. Marina's role is often little more than dispute moderator.

"She might," Jackson admits, "but I can guarantee my deal is better for you."

"One Teleportation scroll costs more than most laborers earn in a year," says Barsi. "Your sister has the means to get me dozens upon request. I only need to give her a compelling reason to cooperate."

Laughter bursts out of Jackson.

"Last chance for an easy deal," he says.

Try not to kill them. Some may still be of use.

The Shapeshifter attacks first, turning into a bear and taking a mighty swing at Jackson.

On his own, the fight would have ended right there, but the Dark Man's presence provides heightened reflexes as well as senses. Jackson deftly steps aside, moving only far enough to avoid being struck. Calling three scrolls from the Veil, he activates the first. A shield appears around him just before two lightning bolts slam into him. Something that should have knocked him senseless merely tingles across his skin.

He feels the Minder's clumsy efforts to press down upon his thoughts and slow his reflexes, but it's like a person off in the distance shouting to be heard. He ignores the attack for now. The two wielding staffs twirl them in complicated patterns, then charge. Jackson spins away from the first strike, gripping the weapon as it passes to the left of his body. Though tempted to yank the staff free, he chooses the more impressive course and squeezes the wooden weapon.

It shatters.

The attacker cries out in dismay and rage.

Jackson continues the spin, driving his left elbow up under the man's chin.

The scream morphs as outrage gets swiftly replaced by pain, then cuts off as the man loses consciousness.

The second staff smashes into Jackson's chest. The shield lets him shrug off the blow, but he's annoyed that it landed. Gripping the weapon, he pulls right then strikes back, rotating his wrist, so the blow lands fully on the man's left leg.

Forming a fierce falcon, the Shapeshifter screeches a battle cry and aims for Jackson's face, claws extended.

Reaching out, Jackson conjures a heavy blanket right in front of the falcon. The bird blunders straight into the trap. The bird's shriek changes to a man's grunt as the figure hits the ground and transforms.

By this time, Barsi has conjured several fireballs and holds them ready for when an opening presents itself. The Destroyers hold fresh lightning bolts, but they too refrain from casting them.

Barsi holds out a hand, turning the lull into a temporary truce. He brightens the fireballs and moves them into the air above, increasing the amount of light significantly. Two energy orbs join the fireballs, changing the quality of the light from orange-yellow to white.

"I may have underestimated you," says Barsi, "but if you can best us, why do you need us? Surely this woman you wish dead is even less of a match."

It is time.

"I need a volunteer," says Jackson. Before Barsi can respond, Jackson moves to the unconscious man and kneels. Placing a hand upon the man's right shoulder, Jackson braces for the unpleasantness to come. The sharp pain that charges through his hand steals his breath, but he manages not to scream.

The Dark Man's essence leaves Jackson in a rush.

His victim wakes long enough to utter a long, desperate shout before slumping over dead.

The other men look on with a mixture of horror and awe. Shock keeps them relatively quiet until the dead man sits up, and they go perfectly still and silent.

Jackson clutches his dagger nervously and silently preps the second scroll he drew from the Veil. It's another shield. If they attack now with any sort of coordination, he could fall in the battle. He still has the third scroll, a nullifier, but he won't use that unless he's truly desperate. It will prevent his attackers from using magic, but it will also interfere with his ability to conjure.

Thankfully, the focus shifts away from him.

Slowly, the body stiffens and rises, rotating until it reaches a standing position.

"You have witnessed my power through one man," says the Dark Man. "He has been a loyal servant and will be rewarded accordingly. Consider this my invitation. Serve me. The other choice is death."

The man with the wounded leg shakes his head, looking dazed.

"You are the Outcast," he declares.

"And you are a criminal," replies the Dark Man. "Thus, an outcast as well. Together, we can be more."

The man shakes his head again.

"I won't serve you."

"Pity." The Dark Man bows his head in acknowledgement of the man's choice. "Kill him."

Jackson feels the impulse to act press upon his mind, but he barely has time to draw his dagger out of the pocket.

Two lightning bolts, one from each Destroyer, strike the man from either side.

He collapses.

"No more!" cries Barsi. Lowering himself to the ground, he bows before the Dark Man. "What is it you wish, Master?"

"My servant spoke truth," intones the Dark Man. "You will plan to kill Gabriella Polani. She stands in the way of something I desire. No trace of the deed can lead back to him."

"What of my people?" asks Barsi.

"Take the Destroyers and the Minder and go," says the Dark

Man. "No harm will come to you, but keep a low profile until I have need of you."

Sending the Shapeshifter a guilty look, Barsi and the others leave via the last Teleportation scroll Jackson gave the man. Without their magic sustaining them, both the fireballs and the energy orbs wink out. Only moonlight remains until Jackson conjures an Illumination scroll. Once activated, four energy orbs take up positions around the three figures in the courtyard.

Shaking off the blanket Jackson conjured, the Shapeshifter crawls forward on his hands and knees. To Jackson's surprise, he realizes the man is weeping.

"I've sought you so long, Master!" he declares.

"I know, Emilio," says the Dark Man. "I have heard your desire to be useful, and I am here to grant your request. Travel east to the Desolate Mountains. After some training, I will give you the next task. My servant will give you the supplies you need for the journey."

Taking the cue, Jackson calls forth the bundle his master had him prepare ahead of time.

Thanking both the Dark Man and Jackson profusely, the Shapeshifter fashions a makeshift sack out of the conjured blanket and leaves the fort.

Jackson watches the man's exit without comment. Once alone, he addresses the Dark Man.

"What did you mean earlier when you said we're overthinking the situation with Marina?"

No longer needing to impress anybody, the Dark Man lets the borrowed body slump to the ground.

We have sought to make Marina quit cities completely, but as previously discussed, she has a wanderer's heart. We need do nothing more than encourage her to go on more mercy missions to remote villages. Then, we can collect her at any moment.

The simplicity stuns Jackson. He prepares to go to Fort Medron to think on the matter.

Take the bodies with you.

Used to such orders, Jackson opens a tear in the Veil wide enough to hold both bodies. He then pictures the target fort's combat arena and finishes the conjuring transfer. The effort leaves him drained but satisfied.

Your skills have improved much since acquiring your former master's ancient manuscripts. Well done.

Chapter 10:
No Use

Gathering Hall, Village of New Haven
Four and a half years after the marriage of Gabriella and Marcus
(Christa's twins are five and a half years old)

Sinking onto the floor, Marina leans back against a crate of bandages and stretches her legs out in front, letting the cool floorboards soothe the ache in her calves. Her feet tell her many hours have passed since her last break. Every other moment since their arrival early this morning has been spent rushing about instructing volunteers and delivering supplies. Raelyn Cordova made her eat something a few hours ago, but even that meal had been consumed on a trek between houses.

Closing her eyes, Marina lets her thoughts wander to the previous day when her apprentice rushed into her office with an urgent request.

Is she still my apprentice?

The question doesn't have a definite answer. They hadn't had much contact since the clinic fire that forced Marina's move from Temperance about two years ago. The sporadic letters and messages exchanged focused on the rebuilding effort. Neither had made a move to formally end the relationship. Marina didn't dare set foot in Temperance, for fear of endangering the work, and Raelyn kept too busy for many social visits to Outreach.

Nothing like a crisis to bring people together.

An outbreak of Brasier's Disease was devastating villages near the Purity Plains. The Arkonai High Council put out a general call for Healers, but few huntsmen could answer the call immediately, since they tended to work in far-flung corners of the continent. Raelyn's father wanted to go, but she—and her mother—didn't want him to take the risk since it seems to strike older people harder. He agreed to continue the work in Temperance on the sole condition that Raelyn ask Marina for help.

In truth, much of Marina's energy since moving to Outreach went into preparing such relief efforts. The vast Castaloni holdings included companies focused on shipping, storage, and creating magic scrolls. With her guidance, the managers were finally starting to work together more cohesively.

Having Transportation scrolls that functioned like Teleportation scrolls for large quantities of supplies had been Jack's idea. Due to the extreme rarity of them, this was Marina's first time using one. They weren't even ready to sell the scrolls yet because creating one required a very skilled Conjurer working through a long, complicated spell. She had yet to decide if she liked them but silently admitted that today's work had been much easier because of the Transportation scroll. She suspected there would be high demand for them whenever they were released to the public because the ability to move large inanimate objects across long distances had many applications.

Before Marina can ponder the point further, a warm body settles beside her and wraps arms around her waist. She returns the embrace even as she tilts her head to see who it is.

"Hello, Riona," she greets. "I'm glad for the company, but what brings you over here? Don't you want to play with the others?"

The girl shrugs, shakes her head, and scoots even closer. According to one of the village elders, Riona hasn't spoken much since her parents fell ill almost a week ago. Since New Haven's sole quarantine cabin is occupied, the child's parents sent her to stay in the Gathering Hall with several of the older village children in much of the same situation. Guessing the little girl means to stay a while, Marina pulls the child onto her lap and lets her snuggle.

A sense of longing sweeps over her as she rests her chin on the child's head. For the first time, Marina begins to understand why some Saroth women spend the first month bonding to their children, at least the firstborn.

I guess it gets complicated after that.

With things finally settling into a normal rhythm, her thoughts turn to the possibility of having a child. Many conversations tell her Daniel won't stand for an isolation month. Aside from her safety, she's never seen anything upset her husband like the brief visit with Gabriella soon after Katrina's birth. It would be nice in some respects, but she sees Daniel rarely enough to make any time together precious. Besides, years living around Arkonai has taught her that most of the men have a deeply ingrained need to protect their families.

That is one thing I envy them.

Her father had never been purposefully distant, but he loved the details of keeping the various companies improving and expanding. That kept him away a lot.

Seeking a happier line of thought, Marina wonders how her adopted sister fares raising a toddler. Her brother, Gabriel, visits the Polani estate regularly and keeps Marina informed of the latest news.

Gabriel and Gabriella. They always were inseparable.

Even during the days Gabriella's last name was Ricci, Gabriel spent countless hours playing with her, despite the age gap.

A giggle from Riona makes Marina look down, ending her idle musings. She follows the child's line of sight out to where Gabriel entertains some of the village children. Her heart warms as she watches him scurry over and under benches and children in squirrel form.

Laughter and squeals erupt from the children. They scatter, darting in every direction to escape the crazy squirrel. As usual, Gabriel has taken great care with the details of fur and features in the creature form. This version sports a beige body with bright red fur along the bushy tail.

Better stop this before somebody gets hurt.

As the thought completes, a boy trips and falls headlong toward a bench.

Still in squirrel form, Gabriel leaps and initiates the change to human form. His body elongates as the transformation magic takes over. The boy's head plows into Gabriel's stomach. By the time they land, the child's alarmed cry has changed to one of delight.

Scrambling to her feet, Marina tucks Riona against her side and rushes to check on her brother.

He's short of breath but grinning madly.

"Can we do it again?" asks the boy, leaping to his feet. His Bereft accents gives the question a rolling cadence.

Gabriel dutifully assumes his squirrel body again but freezes when he spots Marina.

"I think there's been enough excitement." Marina's tone contains a calm she doesn't feel. Her heart races, resulting in sharp chest pain. She clutches the girl close, letting the child's head rest on her shoulder. "We should probably settle down for the evening."

How did we inherit childminding duties?

Her announcement gets met with a chorus of protests. The children plead and bargain until they realize she won't change her mind. Gabriel takes their side by assuming his wolf form, sitting up straight, and whining.

"You're no help," Marina tells her brother. The words lack bite. She never could stay mad at him.

"How about a story?" asks the Bereft boy who had crashed into Gabriel. "Can we have a story?"

The children immediately take up the cause. Even Riona lifts her head off Marina's shoulder long enough to nod in agreement. The move nearly causes Marina to drop the child.

"What say you, Gabriel?" ask Marina, adjusting her grip on Riona. "Think you can handle a story that won't bring down the building?"

Her brother shifts back to human form, but before he can reply, the main door slams open. A young man sprints inside. The children tighten ranks around Marina and Gabriel.

"Lady Marina!" he calls. Skidding to a halt before the tiny crowd, Callen struggles to catch his breath and report his news. "Brotherhood riders. You must hide!"

Two more men enter behind Callen. Marina recognizes the older one as Elder Silas Ikrest. She's never seen the other man, but his hostile expression tells her enough about his beliefs to be wary.

"Stand aside, huntsman," orders the elder. He raises his hands in a calming gesture.

Callen summons a short sword to hand, but he doesn't raise it.

"Take the children into the back and stay with them." Marina reinforces the order by handing Riona over to Gabriel.

Without arguing, he grabs the nearest child's hand and starts herding the lot away from the standoff.

"Go with them, my lady," says Callen, keeping his attention on the two men. "I will protect you."

"Hand her over peacefully, or we'll burn the village down." The stranger's quiet announcement and cold gray eyes root Marina in place.

"This is wrong." Callen's eyes drill the declaration into the village elder.

"Aye," agrees Elder Silas, "but we canna fight them, lad." His agitation thickens his accent. "We need their protection."

"My father—"

"Isn't here." Elder Silas cuts Callen off.

The sound of many horses brings a smile to the Brotherhood man.

"You'll change sides eventually," he says to Callen.

"My lady, please retreat," says Callen. "I may have to fight them, and I don't want to hurt you."

"Do you know why they want me?" Marina inquires, touched by the man's concern. She reviews everything she knows about him. His father owns much of the surrounding farmland. He and his family spend most of their time in the city of Cardeth. They visit small villages like New Haven several times a year to check on the people who work their family lands.

"We have unfinished business," says a confident male voice.

Marina senses something familiar about the voice but cannot place it until she sees the blond man enter, flanked by several men. The empty space fills quickly with Arkonai men. Each figure wears typical huntsman clothes. In addition, they have dark green cloaks with the cowls raised.

"Huntsman Garok," Marina says, working hard to keep her tone pleasant. Their brief encounter many years ago had not gone well. The passage of time seems not to have diminished his irrational hatred of her people.

"It's Huntmaster Garok now, but I wouldn't expect a Saroth to know the difference." He takes three steps forward before Callen's sword brings him to a halt. "Not wise."

When Garok raises his right hand, the Arkonai Brotherhood men conjure weapons. Most are bows or crossbows centered on Callen. A few aim at Marina.

"This land belongs to my father and is under my protection," says Callen. "You have no authority to make demands."

"I'd rather not have to explain your death to your father or your wife and son, but I will if I must," says Huntmaster Garok.

"It's no use," says Elder Silas. "Give it up, lad."

"Da!" A tow-headed child only slightly older than Katrina darts in and flings himself at Callen.

"Tellen." Moving the sword aside, Callen stoops and catches the boy, holding him with one arm as he raises his sword again. "What are you doing here?" Distress makes the question sound wispy.

"Wonderful," says Garok. "Now I won't have to explain to your family. They'll get to experience your fate."

A Brotherhood man enters with a brown-haired woman in tow. A thick rope circles her neck and attaches to her wrists which are bound in front of her chest. Tears of pain and fear pool in her eyes.

Callen's rigid posture identifies the woman for Marina. His sword arm lowers to his side. He drops the weapon, and it disappears into the Veil.

Marina touches his right elbow as she moves up beside him.

"It's all right," she whispers, blinking back tears. "Thank you for trying."

She only makes it a half-step further before Callen catches her left hand.

"You'll die," he says hoarsely.

"Only if the One wills it," Marina replies. Despite the words, she expects Garok to fulfill the prediction soon. A chill settles upon her as she reads the contempt and hatred etched into his features. Feeling her knees weaken, Marina pulls her hand free of Callen's grasp and kneels. She steadies herself by focusing on a spot near Garok's feet. "I don't know why you hate me, but if my life is what you require, take it."

Hands pull Marina to her feet.

Garok snaps his fingers, and the rope binding Callen's wife releases her.

The woman draws several shaky breaths and stares miserably at Marina. She blinks several times, releasing helpless tears. A bright red line mars the woman's neck.

The enchanted rope loops around Marina's left wrist before doing the same to her right wrist. When her hands are drawn together, the binding tightens painfully. Next, the rope draws her hands up and pins them to her chest. Finally, it winds around her neck twice, squeezing hard enough to make her cough. She draws several shallow, inadequate breaths. Only the hands supporting her elbows keep her standing.

"Stop it!" Callen shouts. "You have her. There's no reason to be cruel."

The Brotherhood men shift position, turning her so she can see Callen. He stands holding his son just beyond a line of six swords leveled at his gut, looking mad enough to charge into them.

Marina tries to shake her head, but the enchanted rope prevents movement.

"If I didn't have more important plans to enact, I'd spill your traitor's blood right now," says Huntmaster Garok. "But it would be a shame for her to die before I want her to."

The rope loosens enough for Marina to breathe normally. While grateful for the small favor, she's aware the situation hasn't changed much. Garok's voice still holds many dark promises.

Chapter 11:
Delaying Tactic

Home of Daniel and Marina, City of Outreach
Same Day
(Christa's twins are five and a half years old)
"You left her." Daniel hardly recognizes the cold, dead voice as his own. Only years of self-control training keep him from punching Marina's younger brother.

"I didn't know!" Gabriel's distress manifests in a series of shapeshifts from beetle to wolf to squirrel and back to human. He finishes the cycle in a kneeling position. "I was hiding the children. When I returned, the Brotherhood men were gone, and so was my sister. Only the elder, Huntsman Callen, and his family remained. Elder Silas gave me the scrolls to deliver."

Daniel's furious gaze lands on the crumpled scroll still in his grasp. He doesn't need to read it again. The words still scald his mind.

Twelve hours to surrender.

"Did you inform Marcus and Gabriella yet?" he asks. If the ransom only involved him, he would already be in the village of New Haven, but Huntmaster Garok demanded Marcus's life as well as Daniel's.

I'll be there shortly.

Gabriella's tense thought sails through Daniel's head. A change in Gabriel's expression says Gabriella must also be addressing the Shapeshifter. He shakes his head vigorously.

"I want to stay with Daniel," Gabriel declares. "I'm going after

73

Marina."

Send Gabriel to our estate in Jorash. He can help Marcus make some arrangements. We think this might be the move you've been waiting for concerning Lord Ravine.

A silent demand for a better explanation goes nowhere. Leaps of logic from Minders are nothing new to Daniel but worry for Marina makes reasoning difficult. Guessing Gabriella doesn't want to continue the discussion until they're alone, Daniel seizes Gabriel's arm and pulls him toward the door.

"Go to Jorash," Daniel orders, shoving the younger man across the threshold.

"Please let me help," Gabriel begs.

"Marcus needs you more than I do right now," says Daniel. "If we're going to rescue Marina, we'll need certain scrolls. You're the best chance we have of getting them."

"I'm not," says Gabriel, "but I know who is." Taking his wolf form, Gabriel dashes away.

Daniel stares at his retreating form until the Shapeshifter rounds a corner and disappears. As he starts shutting the door, a new figure appears in the distance. A solid stream of thoughts hits Daniel as he recognizes the rapidly approaching figure as Gabriella.

I'm so sorry, Daniel. We'll get her back. I promise. Marcus and I think Lord Ravine's responsible. He knows you're getting close to the money. He might even bring you right to it before trying to kill you.

Before Daniel can absorb the thoughts completely, Gabriella slams into him, knocking him back a step. The tight embrace carries the whole of her fear and helplessness. Releasing him, Gabriella spins and closes the door. Next, she clears the kitchen table of some scrolls, a fruit basket, and the remains of Daniel's evening meal.

"Why do you think Lord Ravine is involved?" Daniel asks. "And what are you doing?"

"Lie down on the table," Gabriella instructs. "I'm going to try to use your Seeker Gifts to find Marina."

"I thought you could already tap into her thoughts," says Daniel.

"I can," Gabriella confirms, "but that's not going to help us if Marina doesn't know where they took her. Your connection to her is much deeper than mine, and you're a Seeker. If we can find the location, we can send the proper help." She glares at Daniel. "I am not blindly going to send you or my husband into a trap."

"He's willing to go? The League is going to let him go?" Daniel can't keep the surprise out of his voice.

"Of course, he's willing to go. We love her." Gabriella draws a deep breath to keep from crying. "And we are not telling the Tariku League yet because they would never let it happen. We will do everything in our power to make the pair of you trackable, but there are dozens of things that can go wrong. We must gather every scrap of information we can right now."

Daniel lets a brief silence linger to give Gabriella a chance to master her emotions.

"You never answered the question about Lord Ravine," he prompts, setting the threatening scroll on a counter. "Why do you think he stands behind the plot?"

"The demand for Marcus," Gabriella answers. "Your investigation into the Hunting Guild's stolen money is the only motive that explains taking Marina and forcing your surrender."

"What about simple hatred," Daniel says bitterly. "My people are good at that."

Gabriella sinks onto a chair at the table.

"The Brotherhood does not represent your people, Daniel." Gabriella lets some of her tears fall. When she speaks again, her tone is soft and haunted. "If this were only about hatred, you would not have received a scroll, only her body."

"Why does he tolerate them?" Daniel demands, not expecting an answer from her.

"Who are you talking about?" Gabriella wonders.

"Jordan." Daniel pours his frustration into uttering his friend's name. "He's Supreme Huntmaster. He has the authority to hunt them down!"

Gabriella gives him a look that mixes compassion and pity.

Knowing she's likely to share her thoughts soon anyway, he waves for her to speak.

"He's a politician in a very difficult position," Gabriella points out. "I heard he even cut off contact with his wife to appease the extremists. He's not worth your anger." She motions to the table. "Please, lie down. We have much to do."

"He's a fool," Daniel mutters, following the instruction. "Christa deserves better."

"We do a lot of difficult things to protect the people we love," Gabriella notes.

Daniel detects a strange, unidentifiable emotion in her voice but dismisses the feeling when she explains her intentions.

"I'm going to touch your head to aid the connection with your mind." Gabriella's voice gains strength as her focus shifts to the work. "Try to relax. The more you fight me, the longer it will take. If this works, you will feel like you're tapping into one of your Gifts. It's likely nothing will happen, but at the very least, I believe I can connect your spirits."

Gabriella doesn't tell him to use the time to say goodbye, but the notes of dread carry the message anyway. Her cool fingers touch his temples while her palms rest against the sides of his head.

Not wanting to stare aimlessly at the ceiling, Daniel closes his eyes. Though Gabriella usually speaks through Marina or Marcus, her light, skillful touch upon his thoughts feels natural. First, she suppresses the panic preventing him from thinking clearly. Next, Gabriella scans his surface thoughts and organizes the dozens of partial plans into several actionable scenarios. Finally, she reaches for his Seeker Gifts and merges them with her Minder powers.

Daniel's first instinct is to protect his Gifts, but he manages to lower his mental defenses and open his spirit enough to let Gabriella work. To test the connection, she reaches out toward her home in Jorash, seeking to find Marcus or Gabriel Castaloni. After a few seconds of fumbling, they lock onto Marcus's presence in his second-floor study. Pleased but not willing to declare success yet, Gabriella directs the Gift out, trying to locate Corabelle Castaloni.

Why search for Marina's mother?

There are roughly a dozen locations she frequents near here or somewhere in Caramore. Since I am familiar with them, it should let us know if the magic will let us stretch that far before we attempt to locate Marina.

The close connection between their minds lets Daniel sense Gabriella's weariness. She once likened using another's magic Gifts as trying to lift heavy objects with only one hand, doable but difficult.

Images flash behind his closed eyes then fade quickly. He sees the Castaloni estate in Outreach, then the ones in Jorash and Dominance. Nothing alerts him to Corabelle's presence. Gabriella takes them to a variety of meeting chambers for the Tariku League. A warm sensation spreads throughout Daniel's chest as the search lands them in a very small conference room within the Academy of Arts and Sciences. Aware of the confirmation, Gabriella ends the search.

One more time. Have you been to New Haven?

A long time ago. Why?

I could point it out on a map, but your familiarity will help us locate it quickly. I can't do this much longer. Every second matters.

Reaching out with their combined Gifts, Gabriella guides them toward the village of New Haven. Since Daniel had stepped foot there, his Seeker Gifts automatically marked the location, letting them latch onto the place. From there, they rely more heavily upon Seeker senses to feel Marina and follow the trail south toward the Silver Springs.

The connection snaps.

Gabriella moans and removes her hands from Daniel's head.

Sitting up quickly leaves him lightheaded, but concern for Gabriella pushes him past the discomfort. He gets up and reaches her in time to keep her from tumbling out of the chair. After steadying her, Daniel grabs a cloth and dips it in a water bucket then wrings it out. Returning to Gabriella, Daniel uses the damp cloth to brush aside strands of dark hair and clean her sweaty face.

"Don't." Gabriella's expression declares her new fears.

Placing the cloth on the table, Daniel leans over and kisses her hair.

"When you're strong enough, go home and have Marcus report the situation to the Tariku League," says Daniel. "They will argue in circles. That will buy us time. I'll place a mark on myself. That's not the way the Gift is supposed to work, but I believe in you. I'm going to my wife. Come save us if you can. If you can't, pray for us."

How will you find them?

"I'll take a traveler's portal to New Haven and speak with the elders," Daniel replies. "Those were the instructions in the scroll."

I thought you could teleport directly to somebody.

"Only if I'm under contract or very special circumstances." Daniel fervently hopes it doesn't come to that. If that portion of his Gift engages, it will mean the danger facing Marina has turned deadly.

Wait until we have a plan.

"I'm not going to leave her alone with them," Daniel declares. When the wave of helpless anger abates, a new thought occurs to him. "After informing the Tariku League, contact the High Council. Jordan may be mostly useless, but he needs to know how far the Brotherhood huntsmen have strayed."

If you let me rest, I can try to follow you from New Haven to wherever they take you.

"They know of my Gifts," Daniel says. "They will probably have their own Seeker present to prevent such a course of action. You'll have to find my mark once they let their guard down."

Go then. Marcus will follow as soon as possible.

Daniel considers trying to convince his friends to stay in a safe place, but he understands their need to help. A similar feeling pulses through him.

The plan he laid out for Gabriella unfolds as predicted, right down to the precautions against his Seeker Gifts. As he steps out of the traveler's portal in New Haven, he's greeted by a dozen Brotherhood huntsmen. A single energy orb illuminates the area next to the portal, but Daniel can sense each foe.

"Where is your Saroth companion?" demands the leader.

"He is delayed," Daniel answers. "His council must give him permission to leave Caramore."

A short discussion takes place in hushed tones before the leader speaks again.

"Will you submit to a confining spell?" asks the leader.

"If I must," says Daniel.

"Yes or no," snaps the man. "You must satisfy the consent clause."

"Yes. I will submit to a confining spell."

"Good answer."

A wave from the leader sends the Brotherhood men into a flurry of movement. Two Guardians use enchanted ropes to bind his hands together and pin his arms in place against his side. Another man reads the confining spell off a scroll while somebody else holds a scroll up for Daniel to see.

"Read the spell," orders the leader.

Daniel does so. It's a standard deep sleep spell. As he finishes, Daniel drops to his knees and silently prays he'll see Marina when he awakens.

Chapter 12:
Little Drama

Jackson's Study, Fort Medron
Same day
(Christa's twins are five and a half years old)
Your brother will be calling shortly.

Jackson leans back in his chair and rubs at his aching eyes. He's been studying August Polani's commentary on Darkland creatures for many hours.

"What does he want?" He needs a break, but a conversation with Gabriel would not be his first choice for a diversion.

He's come to ask for your help with a little drama I'm arranging. Render the aid.

Although he refrains from groaning, Jackson tenses. His mind fixes on other things the Dark Man has referred to as *little dramas*. The meeting with Barsi, which boiled down to recruiting a new servant for his master, and firebombing Marina's clinic in Temperance were only two examples.

His Keeper's pendant gets warmer and lights up, glowing green briefly to announce a call from Gabriel.

"What can I—"

Gabriel unleashes words before Jackson can finish the question.

"Jack! I need your help. Marina's been kidnapped. Daniel will surrender to buy time. Marcus is with the Tariku League now. He'll get some volunteers to mount a rescue, but you're the only one who can deliver a Teleportation scroll to them."

"What about Mother?" Jackson inquires. "She's a Conjurer.

Have her call one from the Veil."

"There aren't any there!" Gabriel cries. "After the shipment to Jorash disappeared, we moved the ones held in the Veil to warded storage facilities in Outreach and Kaltan City. I can get to either by traveler's portal, but there's no time to deliver them. They need to go to the Academy in Dominance right away."

If Marina and Daniel die—

I need them alive for now.

"Please, Jack. Save her," Gabriel babbles. "Mother's in no condition to retrieve the scrolls, and I'd need at least an hour to get them from the vault in Outreach and another hour to take them to the Academy. The One gave you the ability to Conjure yourself. We need that to save Marina."

Accept the job before I must kill him for being one of Kailon's slave boys.

"How many do you need?" Jackson asks.

"Two, if you can find them," says Gabriel. "I know the shipping headquarters in Outreach should have one, but Kaltan City may be out. They recently fulfilled an order of ten for the city council. Mother said she'd work on more, but it's a long spell. I don't like the toll it takes on her. We're having two Conjurers trained so we can increase the output, but it'll be months before they're ready."

"Fine."

He's exhausting to talk to.

"You'll do it?" Gabriel sounds stunned. "Thank you—"

Jackson cuts the connection before Gabriel can finish heaping praises on him.

"Why am I saving my sister, who I eventually need to kill?" Jackson wonders. Leaning on his desk, he stands to better facilitate his next move. It's possible to conjure his body from a seated position, but that often leaves him off balance when he arrives at his destination.

Because she is the best way to control Daniel Saveron.

"Aren't there other Seekers who can help?" Jackson asks.

For most of their relationship, the Dark Man has fixated on Daniel and Marina.

None with his skill set and magical Gifts. Daniel is a Seeker who can sense both living beings and objects. Most others are highly skilled at one and only minimally capable of the other. He can fight reasonably well, read a room's history, and connect to Minders. If he wasn't so tainted by the light, I would recruit him.

"What are you trying to find?" Jackson presses.

Run your errand.

"I don't have to," says Jackson. "I still have the ones meant to pay Barsi."

Hold two back. He will need them to get into the Polani estate. If you can acquire more for him later, do so. If you cannot, he will accept some other form of payment.

"Which room at the Academy should I go to?"

Aim for the portal room. The wards will direct you there anyway.

Jackson pictures the place, opens a tear in the Veil, and steps inside. The place he appears in makes him nervous. It's like stepping off a cliff and standing on inky black air. Moving swiftly across this land of mist and twisting shadows, Jackson opens a new hole in the Veil and enters the portal room at the Academy of Arts and Sciences in Dominance.

Two portal guards watch him carefully, ceremonial spears held in a position just shy of threatening.

Jackson's mother embraces him tightly before stepping back, still gripping his shoulders.

"Do you have it?" Her expression and tone reek of worry.

"I do," he answers stiffly. Irritation flares, warming his chest. He hasn't seen Mother this worried since the months leading up to his father's death.

You'd think she'd be used to Marina disappearing.

Give her the scrolls.

The Dark Man sounds exasperated.

Jackson does so and has the pleasure of seeing relief wash over her face.

Corabelle turns the Teleportation scrolls over to Adaram Serco. The Nokarti Assassin bows to her and races out of the room.

"Come," says Corabelle. "We will watch the proceedings in the Observatory."

An unexpected thrill touches Jackson. His tutors mentioned the place when discussing the Academy's history and significance, but he never thought he'd get to see it. His mother sets a brutal walking pace as she leads him through many corridors and training rooms. He expects to head up to one of the towers, but instead, his mother opens a door leading to deeper levels. The steep staircase winds down in dizzying circles, but they only descend two levels before traversing another hallway to a different staircase. As Jackson's legs start to ache, his mother steps through into a spacious room leading to several smaller ones.

As they enter, a young woman steps forward and bows.

"Greetings, Lady Corabelle and Master Jackson. I am Navina. My master and several others are waiting for you in Isolation Chamber 2. Please follow me."

The woman leads them into a small room already crowded with people and directs them to a place off to the left side.

"Master Taymore has given me leave to explain things if necessary," says Navina in a hushed tone. "Have you been to the Observatory before?"

"I have, but my son has not," says Jackson's mother.

Jackson can guess what's happening, but he finds Navina's voice pleasant enough. He listens carefully as she explains the setup and people present.

"When we receive the signal, Master Taymore will begin the Vision Cast," Navina explains. "Apprentice Leila, Lady Tabitha, Master Doran, and Apprentice Emilio are present to lend him mental strength as necessary."

Jackson stares hard at the last Minder introduced, but the three energy orbs above dim significantly before he can investigate the sense of familiarity about the man.

He is nobody. Pay attention.

The Minders sit on cushions arranged in a semi-circle with Master Taymore in the center.

"Master Taymore will begin by setting up a frame with the focusing crystals," says Navina. "This narrows the scope of the Vision Cast but allows the images to be clearer. Viewers find the scenes less distracting when the images appear in one place."

"How will he find them?" asks Mother.

"Master Marcus wears a mark," answers Navina. "It's something he and Master Daniel developed a while ago so we could monitor missions and provide adequate support."

"Why is Marcus involved?" Mother's worry sounds more pronounced with this second question. "Surely, you could follow Daniel if he wore such a mark."

"Yes, Lady Corabelle," confirms Navina, "but he is Arkonai. The Tariku League would not intervene to save him, not in those lands. If they were close to Kaltan City, Outreach, or even Temperance, maybe, but those villages are on Arkonai lands."

"Marcus is bait," Jackson comments.

"We were asked to observe and report back to the Council," says Navina. "They will make the final decision, but they are interested in your opinion, my lady."

"This could start a war," Jackson's mother whispers.

Is that what you want?

Eventually, but not until I can maintain a presence on Aeris. That is the current goal. Letting Arkonai zealots kill your sister would interfere with that plan. Hence, you are helping to launch this daring rescue.

A thought occurs to Jackson.

Why couldn't the Tariku League save Marina without Marcus Polani? She's the head of significant business interests. The holdings won't collapse without her, but they would be harmed. There should be clauses about dealing with kidnappers that bring the matter to the Council.

There are such clauses, but the Brotherhood asked for no monetary ransom, only the lives of Daniel and Marcus. These fools lack imagination and already stole enough wealth for seven lifetimes. They are seeking to protect it by eliminating the pair best suited for finding them. I don't care what happens to Marcus, but as previously noted, I need Daniel alive.

Jackson's head pulses painfully as he tries to understand.

Why bother putting Marina in danger? You had to know Daniel would play the fool and answer any challenge, even if it merely means they get to die together.

It is not about Marina and Daniel. It is about ending the Brotherhood, making the Arkonai Hunting Guild independent once more, and breaking the ties between Marcus and Daniel. Watch and learn, my young servant.

Jackson returns his attention to the center in time to see a disturbing scene form within the rectangle created by four focusing crystals.

Marina stands tied to a wooden beam, which sticks up out of a crude, makeshift platform. Ropes bind her hands above her head and secure her waist, neck, and legs to the pole. Her long black hair flows down over her right shoulder, held in place by a thin leather cord. The Vision Cast view cannot convey her expression, but the platform around her bears several stains.

Is that blood?

Yes. They tried to summon Daniel through her pain, but they misunderstood the nature of that kind of contract. Do not worry. They merely wounded her arms and had a Healer on hand to keep her alive.

Does this concern you?

Anger courses throughout Jackson. He's not sure what to think. Causing Marina pain had dominated his efforts for many years, but since their father's death, an uneasy truce has existed for their mother's sake. Knowing his master's long-term plans, Jackson's aware that one day they will be enemies again, but that doesn't make her current situation easier to witness.

Several dozen hooded figures surround the platform on three sides, brandishing weapons. One man paces back and forth across the tiny elevated space addressing the crowd. Jackson doesn't need to hear the words to gather that the man's stoking their bloodlust. The movements and gestures speak quite plainly.

Two figures lay in unconscious heaps before the platform. Jackson guesses these must be Marcus and Daniel. Telling them apart would be impossible with the top-down perspective afforded by the Vision Cast, but a bright yellow beam shines from the figure to Marina's left.

That must be Marcus.

Jackson spares a second to wonder what manner of magic they wove into the spell that made Marcus trackable.

Catch your mother, please.

The Dark Man's warning barely gives Jackson time to turn and obey. Carefully, he eases her down to her knees.

Her distress gets channeled to him through a fierce grip on his hand.

Navina crouches next to his mother.

"Shall we move you, ma'am?" asks the young Minder.

Mother shakes her head firmly.

"I need to see this."

It's a bad idea, but Jackson doesn't have the heart to tell her so.

Together, he and Navina help his mother to a more comfortable sitting position.

They walked into your little trap. Now, how are you going to keep them alive?

Chapter 13:
Apprentice

Arkonai Brotherhood Camp near the Silver Springs
Same day
(Christa's twins are five and a half years old)

Marina's arms ache from being held above her head. For a time, she tried to straighten her arms to take the pressure off her wrists, but the position merely brought a different kind of pain to her shoulders. She hadn't expected to live this long after surrendering to the Brotherhood men who came for her in New Haven.

She tries not to think about the situation and how much worse it's gotten over the course of a few hours. However, concern for Daniel and Marcus keeps the worry fresh.

At first, Marina expected to have her head shaken loose while riding on the back of a horse, but the ordeal passed quickly enough to make her suspect the use of magic. The jostling during the trip caused the ropes to cut into her neck. Next, she had been dumped into a small tent while still bound. When a man finally cut the ropes free, he led her out to this platform and slashed both of her arms in a doomed attempt to get Daniel to teleport. The tactic failed, so Garok had sent men back to New Haven to wait for Daniel's surrender. Mercifully, Garok had ordered a Healer to tend the wounds and left her alone until men arrived with Daniel. Then, he gave her a detailed description of how his people deal with traitors. Only the arrival of more men with Marcus made him switch to railing against the Saroth, the inept High Council, and the One for failing the Arkonai people.

Leaning back against the rough pole, Marina closes her eyes and tries to block the latest round of Garok's lengthy speech. He's been feeding the crowd nonsense for several minutes.

She prays silently.

Father, protect us. We need you now more than ever. Let Daniel and Marcus live. Protect our hearts from hating our enemies. We were not meant to be enemies. Change Garok and his master and each of these men. Show them that acts of violence can never purchase peace.

Her heart continues to plead for her husband and her friend until silence falls over the crowd. The shift causes Marina to open her eyes. At first, she doesn't detect any change. Most Brotherhood men stand outside the circle of light cast by a single energy orb placed above the platform where she stands and the area immediately in front of it. Most men bear a weapon, but a few carry torches, providing an outline to their ranks. She can see enough to know of their presence without being able to distinguish faces.

The shadowy forms part.

Two men separate from the crowd, dragging something between them.

Marina's heartbeats quicken with renewed dread as she recognizes the something as a person. Though dressed similarly to the Brotherhood men, the prisoner's slight build sets him or her apart.

The men push their captive down to a kneeling position between Daniel and Marcus, who still lie where they were dropped.

"How dare you interrupt my fine speech." The mock offense in Garok's tone draws a chuckle from the crowd. "Who is this wretch you've set before me?"

"Found her with the new recruits," answers the man holding firmly to the figure's left shoulder.

The other man tugs the figure's hood off, letting long blond hair tumble free.

A hard shove knocks the woman face-first to the ground, but Marina has seen enough. A soul-deep ache fills her. Tears sting her eyes. She tugs futilely against the wrist restraints. Having never fully recovered from a magical injury many years ago, her right wrist feels only added pressure. Her left wrist feels every fiber of the coarse rope punishing her efforts. Part of her welcomes the physical pain as a counterpoint to the terror of what's to come.

Raelyn.

Murmurs rise from the crowd, but Garok silences them with a raised hand.

Raelyn slowly gets to her knees and looks up, defiance etched into every feature.

Marina's heart lurches. She wants to warn the young woman, but most of her effort goes into controlling the urge to sob.

"My dear lady, I do believe you're lost," Garok comments.

He motions again, and the two escorts sweep in and yank her upright. The man near Marcus kicks his still form aside to gain room to stand near Raelyn. Jumping down from the platform, Garok approaches Raelyn with a predator's smooth grace. He eases forward, nearly stepping on Daniel.

"I require some space," Garok states.

The men holding Raelyn release her arms and hurry to drag Daniel and Marcus off to the sides.

"That's much better." Garok executes a slow circle around Raelyn. "I don't believe we've ever formally met. I would remember such beauty, I'm sure." When his circuit brings him back in front of Raelyn, Garok bows. "I am Huntmaster Garok of the Arkonai Brotherhood. May I know your name?"

"Let her go," Raelyn whispers, keeping her gaze fixed on Marina. She blinks, and two tears slip out onto her cheeks.

"Hush now," says Garok, brushing the tears aside with his thumbs. His next words have a sharper edge. "Your grief is misplaced." Retreating a step, Garok whirls and addresses Marina. "You, Saroth. This beautiful creature seems broken. Does she have a name?"

Sensing a trap within the question, Marina hesitates.

With an exaggerated shrug, Garok draws a dagger and contemplates it.

"Well, she can't stay here," he notes. "She'd drive my men crazy."

The Brotherhood men laugh on command before falling eerily silent again.

"Setting her loose in this wilderness would be cruel," Garok continues. "I suppose I'll have to put her down."

"Her name is Raelyn," Marina calls.

Sheathing his dagger, Garok moves to a position halfway between Raelyn and Marina.

"Why would a Saroth know such a beautiful creature?" he wonders, addressing the question to the whole crowd. Garok looks first to Marina and then to Raelyn. Crossing over to the young woman, he picks up her left hand. "Do you have a family name?"

"Cordova," she answers.

"Cordova," Garok repeats slowly. He pats her hand and releases it. "My late uncle may have known a relative of yours, one Emeric Cordova. Any relation?"

"My father," Raelyn replies.

Garok's features take on a shrewd cast.

"The Cordova family line goes back many generations and has been blessed with many Healers," he says. "Tell me, did you inherit these magical Gifts?"

Raelyn nods once.

"Good to know," says Garok. He starts pacing in front of the platform, pretending to be deep in thought. "Are you a traitor?"

"No!" Marina cries, staring hard at her apprentice. Fear makes her strain against the cord holding her neck in place. "Admit to nothing!"

"According to you, yes," Raelyn answers, having found courage in her anger. "Call me what you like. I am not the one cowering in this 'wilderness' as you called it, threatening people who have done nothing to me or you or anybody. They are the finest people I have ever known, and if that makes me a traitor, then I'll say it again. Yes."

Another hand gesture snaps the two escorts back into action. Each man holds one of Raelyn's elbows.

Approaching slowly, Garok raises his hands in a helpless gesture.

"My lady, you have put me in a bind. What shall I tell your father about your death?" His question sounds almost kind.

As her despair finds new, uncharted heights, inspiration strikes Marina.

"Garok. Wait! She's my apprentice. Her faults and flaws are mine to bear."

The announcement causes an uproar as the Brotherhood men voice their opinions.

"She's right," calls a brave man from the crowd. "Let her take a beating before her death."

"Kill the traitor!" cries another man.

Almost a minute passes before Garok can render a ruling.

"You raise an interesting point, Saroth," he concedes. "But that law only applies to Arkonai."

"The Cordova girl is Arkonai, if she speaks truth about her Healing Gift," argues the brave man.

"If her punishment falls to another, then she goes free," Garok argues. "That could cause us a lot of trouble, Seric. How do you propose we deal with that?"

"The law only dictates she be alive when leaving our custody," says Seric, stepping briefly into the light. "It says nothing about where we release her. Both the Ashlands and the Badlands have plenty of dangers that would assure she never makes it back to civilized lands."

"Done." Garok fills the word with finality.

Throwing her full weight against the man to her right, Raelyn breaks free and leaps toward Garok. He shoves her shoulders hard, making her stumble back into the waiting arms of her escorts. Quickly, Garok follows the shove up with a short punch to her left side, just below her ribs. The blow weakens her knees, so the men ease her to the ground to recover.

"Garok, what is going on?" demands a new voice. An older Arkonai man pushes through the crowd and enters the ring formed by the spectators. "Kill the Saroth and the traitors. The men need rest before the journey tomorrow."

The torches jerk upward as the Brotherhood men straighten. Most murmurs are indistinguishable, but Marina hears one man's awed whisper.

"Lord Ravine!"

"One of the traitors is an apprentice to the Saroth woman," Garok explains. "We were discussing her fate."

"Do it quickly," orders Lord Asalor Ravine. "I want the men resting within the hour." Without waiting for a response, the man passes through the crowd again.

This time, they part willingly, creating a narrow path.

Garok seethes.

"We should prove if the girl's a Healer," Seric says.

Releasing a frustrated cry, Garok plucks a throwing dagger from the line attached to his belt and flings it into the upper portion of Marina's right leg.

Expecting such a move, Marina confines her response to a short cry and some quiet tears. A burning sensation radiates from the wound. She's not sure what poison coated the blade, but it works swiftly.

"Cut her down," Garok orders.

Two men dart out of the crowd to obey.

Marina's legs weaken, causing the rope around her neck to tighten.

Seizing Raelyn's shoulder, Garok pulls her up and pushes her toward the platform.

"Heal the wound," he commands.

Catching her balance, Raelyn turns back to Garok.

"Kill me yourself, you coward." Anger renders her words in halting bursts.

"I would gladly, my lady," says Garok with an icy smile, "but all things in order. I'd meant to kill the Saroth in a more dignified manner, but Boseri poison will do the job just fine. It's messier—and far more painful—than an arrow or a sword strike. Heal her or don't. At this point, I don't care."

The men finish dealing with the ropes holding Marina to the pole and lay her on the platform.

Her mind fills with things she should experience soon. Boseri poison causes both painful lesions and paralysis. In most people, it becomes a race between the two symptoms to see which can kill faster. The numbness in her legs says this dose heavily favors paralysis but burning sensations along both arms and across her stomach tell Marina the lesions are not far behind.

Next thing she's aware of is Raelyn kneeling over her, crying. A hand lands on Marina's forehead. A wave of cool peace washes over her, and she has a strong desire to sleep. Something grips her right hand hard, and the burning sensations cease. Finally, the sharp pain in her right leg disappears. A delicate touch falls upon Marina's neck.

"Leave that," calls Garok's voice. "She'll live. I'm convinced you're a Healer."

Lightheaded from the healing magic, Marina can only feebly grasp Raelyn's hand and convey thanks with her eyes.

The young woman still holds the poisoned throwing dagger. Her features harden with determination.

Catching her meaning, Marina forces words to come.

"You heal."

The moment passes.

The dagger clatters onto the wooden platform.

Raelyn leans down and kisses Marina's forehead, raining tears across her face.

"Rest now. It will be over soon," she says.

Garok's men pull Raelyn away before she can say more.

Marina's eyes flutter shut as the urge to sleep intensifies. She loses consciousness before she can think of more than her apprentice's name.

Chapter 14:
Council Politics

Deliverance Hall, City of Bastion
Next day
(Christa's twins are five and a half years old)

"We are glad to hear your wife is recovering well after the eventful evening, Huntsman Seeker," says Supreme Huntmaster Jordan Lekros. "As to time off, your request will be given proper attention in our deliberations. Do you have any final remarks to make before we turn to other testimonies?"

They have heard nothing.

Daniel Saveron stares up at Jordan, hardly recognizing his childhood friend. The carefree, sandy-haired reckless boy has changed into a grave man. He wonders what kind of man Jordan would be without the power and responsibility of being Supreme Huntmaster.

Would he be a better husband and father?

Pushing past the idle question, Daniel ponders his response to the inevitable verdicts. Given past dealings and previous comments in this session, Daniel can predict which way each Council member's vote will go. Lord Frederick Marsh will want to impress Jordan and the senior members, so his vote will join any majority. Huntmaster Emanuel Ibish and Lord Terrence of Cardeth would both have sided with Daniel on many issues, but the Cardeth council member laid down his voting right due to a conflict of interest. His son, Callen, had been threatened by the Brotherhood men who kidnapped Marina. Lord Eric Dillworth and Jordan will both blindly support any stance that proves good for the Arkonai Hunting Guild.

In most matters, Daniel might agree with things that advance Guild interests, but several things about this affair bother his conscience. First, he doesn't trust Lord Asalor Ravine and finds the man's claims of having a silent contract from Christa's uncle completely ridiculous. Second, the notion of questioning the Tariku League's right to send help is insulting and counterproductive to good relations with the Saroth.

Marcus should be home with Gabriella and Katrina, not standing in this place wearing chains.

The chains are ceremonial in nature but a stupid way to exert the council's authority.

Third, they should be scouring cities and villages for more people like Raelyn Cordova rather than questioning her actions. Fourth, he's not comfortable with basing decisions on money, which they will surely do.

Willpower keeps Daniel from storming out. He needs to stay for Marcus and Raelyn. The crowd of spectators appears neutral on their fates, but Daniel knows they can turn in an instant. To focus himself, he sweeps his senses over the spectators. Several presences feel familiar, but he doesn't take the time to identify them.

"We were placed in difficult circumstances," Daniel says. "The Brotherhood huntsmen feared Marcus and me and took measures to control us. We could only participate in the battle after being set free by Saroth agents. The wayward huntsmen underestimated Raelyn and paid dearly for the lapse. I only hope the Council will accept the lesson presented and learn from it."

"Which lesson are you referring to?" asks Huntmaster Eric Dillworth. His voice echoes the contempt apparent in his gaze.

"Not every Arkonai in possession of magical Gifts belongs to the Hunting Guild, nor should they," Daniel answers. For an instant, he pictures what it would be like to practice his Seeker Gifts outside of Guild jobs. He could do it. Even if the Guild blacklisted him from working within Arkonai territory, neutral cities and even Saroth cities would have plenty of work, especially since he'd have no competition.

"But if they are not in the Guild, we cannot control them," argues Huntmaster Dillworth.

"Every major city has a council, and most villages have elders to govern them," says Daniel. "We do not covet that power. Why is this different?"

"Those without proper training can be dangerous," says Lord Terrence, directing the words to Daniel. He then turns to his colleagues. "But there are training grounds not affiliated with the Guild. A little competition is good."

Jordan raises a hand to halt further debate.

"Let us move on to other phases," he says. "Raelyn Cordova of Temperance, we have heard much today but not from you. In your own words, please describe what happened after you drove off the poison inflicted upon Marina Castaloni-Saveron."

"I put her in a deep sleep, so she could heal," says Raelyn. "I fully expected Garok to——"

"Huntmaster Garok," interrupts Huntmaster Dillworth. "Let us not forget that whatever his personal beliefs, he was a Guild member who had earned the rank."

The young Healer tenses.

"*Huntmaster* Garok had just finished torturing my mentor and friend with one of the most vile poisons we know." Raelyn's tone cools considerably. "I feared for my life, but before he had a chance to do anything else, the camp came under attack."

"What did you do during this attack?" asks Jordan.

"I stayed with Marina for most of the time," says Raelyn.

"That is not the testimony Seeker Daniel gave," says Lord Fredrick Marsh of Resilience. "He said——"

"When I saw an opportunity to help, I took it," Raelyn declares. "I won't apologize for that."

"Mind your tone," scolds Dillworth. "Your actions aided in the death of many men, including several respected Guild members. We have the authority to prosecute you for those deaths."

"Peace, Eric. Let her finish," says Jordan. "Describe how you helped the aggressors in the fight."

"Any time a man received a wound grave enough to require healing, I exerted my Gifts to accomplish it and put him to sleep as I did with Marina," Raelyn explains.

"It's brilliant," comments Lord Terrence. "Compassionate yet effective."

"It is an abuse of the Healing Gift," complains Huntmaster Dillworth. "We should not tolerate this."

"Would you have preferred I run them through with a sword like Lord Ravine did?" Raelyn laces the question with venom.

"I have explained my actions," says Lord Asalor Ravine. "I'm sure the Council will vote with wisdom in those matters when the time comes. This is about you, my dear."

His confidence makes Daniel nervous that the man will

somehow talk his way out of the crime. His *explanation* consisted of the silent contract claim, which he knew could never be fully investigated. Gut clenching, Daniel recalls the scene of bound Brotherhood men lying dead in two neat lines.

"I only know that most of the Brotherhood men were alive when I returned to the village of New Haven," says Raelyn. "The Saroth fighters avoided killing blows wherever possible."

"I object," says Huntmaster Dillworth. "She cannot know that."

"Strike the Healer's last statement from the record," Jordan instructs. "I think we've heard enough testimony for now. Let us break for half an hour."

As Jordan's gavel strike makes the recess official, Daniel moves to Raelyn and Marcus. He longs to remove their shackles but doesn't wish to provoke the council when they're so close to a decision.

"Are you all right, my lady?" he asks Raelyn. "We should sit down while we have a chance."

"You needn't fuss, Daniel." The Healer forces a dim smile. "If this doesn't go our way, I'll have plenty of time to sit."

"Well, I could use the rest," says Marcus. "The scribes have abandoned their post. I'm sure they wouldn't mind if we sat a while." He looks to Daniel for confirmation.

"It's allowed," says Daniel.

"Would you care to join me?" Marcus lifts his bound hands enough to present his elbow to Raelyn. Leaning over conspiratorially, he adds, "I think it'll do Daniel's nerves some good."

Daniel wants to voice a witty reply, but his heart's too heavy for the task.

"Might I interrupt those deep thoughts?" inquires a male voice.

Turning toward the speaker, Daniel straightens and bows.

"My apologies, Lord Terrence. I am at your service."

"Before I deliver my message, I wanted to ask if your wife is up to having visitors." Concern lines his face. "I, for one, would very much love the chance to thank the woman who saved my son and his family, and Callen has requested the privilege as well."

"I think she would like that," says Daniel. "Her mother is watching over her currently, but now that we're sure Marina will fully recover, keeping her abed will be difficult."

"I certainly have no wish to overwhelm her," comments Lord Terrence. "Shall I have Callen leave the boy home? Tellen's a good lad, but he can be a bit too lively sometimes."

"Your entire family is welcome at our home, my lord," says Daniel. "We have no children but hope to one day."

"Children are a blessing," says Lord Terrence. His eyes twinkle with mirth. "And grandchildren are even better, but allow me to get to my main point. I was asked to send you to the Supreme Huntmaster's office for a private audience. With my message delivered, I shall take my leave. Good day, Huntsman Seeker."

Daniel's return farewell hits empty air as the Cardeth man swiftly walks away.

Curious, Daniel exits the main chamber and traverses the few hallways until he reaches Jordan's office.

Why would he want to meet with me? Is this even allowed?

The door to Jordan's office stands ajar. The lack of a Pirok Guard tells Daniel this meeting may not be with his friend. As he approaches the door cautiously, a quiet voice reaches out to him.

"Please come in, Daniel," calls Christa Lekros. "I am not supposed to be here. The break will be over shortly, and I need to speak with you."

Before he can overthink the situation, Daniel enters the office. As he clears the door, it closes. He whirls and prepares to draw a weapon from the Veil. An energy orb brightens the room, showing him Christa wearing a plain dress and dark cloak. She extends a hand, which he takes instinctively.

"How is Marina?" Her tone starts out with pure concern then mixes in frustration. "I wanted to visit her, but Jordan won't allow it. Said it was too much exposure."

"I'm sure he only wants to keep you safe," Daniel says, trying not to pry. After an appropriate interval, he releases Christa's hand. "What can I do for you, Lady Christa?"

His formality pains her, but he doesn't know how to comfort her while maintaining proper boundaries. Jordan's office receives regular sweeps. If the Seeker reading the room ever discovered them meeting in private, many uncomfortable questions would arise.

"I put up a privacy spell, so you needn't worry about being caught with me." Christa waves to the floor where several spent scrolls litter the ground. Her mouth forms a half-smile. "And I have no interest in breaking your heart or Marina's."

"Are you sure you're not a Minder?" asks Daniel.

"I don't need such skills to read you, Daniel," says Christa, completing the smile. "You've always had a lousy Challenger face. That's why I liked betting against you when we were children." The grin vanishes completely. "I need your help with Jordan."

"With what?" Daniel wonders, doubtful he can do much of anything to persuade his friend.

"He's a good man," says Christa. "Stubborn, infuriating, and often misguided, but a good man. He needs you to stay in the Guild, and I need you to stay for him."

"What makes you think I would quit?" asks Daniel.

Christa doesn't bother answering directly, but Daniel remembers thinking such thoughts recently.

"The High Council still has good men, but there are many more like Ravine showing up," says Christa. "He will be acquitted soon and eventually welcomed back onto the council."

Daniel's expression conveys his next question.

"I've heard enough private discussions in my home to suspect the deal they're cutting." Christa frowns and presses fingers to her temples. Her grief deepens. "I also have informants in many places. And Jordan is almost as easy to read as you. The council of jackals has trained him well."

"Lord Terrence—"

"Is among the trustworthy men," Christa confirms. "But he's not voting today, and I think that was by design."

"You think the Council arranged for Lord Terrence's family to be threatened?" Daniel doesn't bother hiding his shock.

Christa pulls up her hood and lets her hands fall to her sides.

"Without proof, my beliefs mean absolutely nothing, but I can tell you what the afternoon session will bring."

"Was the whole thing a hoax gone wrong?" Daniel asks.

"I don't think we'll ever know," says Christa.

"Could it have been a power play by Lord Ravine?"

"That is my guess," says Christa. "Council politics have gotten even more dangerous since my uncle's death. If my sources speak truth, you can expect the following: Lord Ravine's acquittal in exchange for the location of the remaining treasury funds. Your leave will be granted. They'll likely even elevate you to the rank of huntmaster and have you train Seekers upon your return. The fate of your Saroth friend and the Healer will hinge upon your answer. They won't forbid you from working with Marcus Polani, but they will also keep you too busy to do so."

Stooping, Christa picks up the spent scrolls and tucks them away in her cloak.

"What should I do?" asks Daniel.

"I cannot tell you what to do, but I beg you to stay for your friends and for Jordan. He may not say it, but he trusts you." Christa holds out a small, sealed scroll. "When you see Marina, please give her my love and this letter."

Daniel accepts the scroll but can find no words to say.

Christa opens the door for him.

"Better return," she says. "I'll slip into the crowd later."

In a daze, Daniel wanders back to the main chamber and waits for the second session to begin. He's disheartened but not completely shocked to witness every one of Christa's predictions come true, right down to veiled threats against Marcus and Raelyn. Though he would prefer to consult with Marina before making any life-altering decisions, Daniel cautiously accepts the new rank and responsibilities.

Chapter 15:
Merciful

Home of Daniel and Marina, City of Outreach
Same day as the trial
(Christa's twins are five and a half years old)

As Corabelle Castaloni reaches to awaken her daughter, she pauses and strokes Marina's right cheek. The young Healer had insisted Marina be roused every few hours to drink a special broth that would combat the dehydration side effect of driving off the Boseri poison.

You look so peaceful. I wish I could preserve that feeling for you.

Resting her hand upon Marina's shoulder, Corabelle indulges in a private moment of despair and worry for her firstborn child. Knowing that her daughter's decision to marry an Arkonai man might arouse anger had not prepared her to see such hatred almost kill her. Only conscious thought keeps her hand from trembling. Poison may have been involved in her husband's death. She did not allow an investigation into the possibility because the knowledge would have destroyed her entire family, thanks to an ancient law about Unforgivable Crimes.

First Antonio. Now you. What will it take to keep you safe?

Pain pricks Corabelle's heart at the realization she truly cannot protect her child from making dangerous decisions.

You always were your father's daughter, at least in spirit. Gentle. Kind. Generous. Always ready to see the good in people.

To control the impulse to cry, Corabelle tallies the features on her daughter's face and assigns them to Antonio or herself. In truth, there's little of her husband reflected in the shape of Marina's nose, cheeks, or mouth. He used to tease that if not for the girl's brilliant blue eyes, he'd think he had no part in making her. Suddenly anxious to see her eyes, Corabelle squeezes Marina's shoulder.

As the Healer predicted, Marina snaps awake instantly, flinches, and grips the blanket hard. The pure terror in her eyes hurts Corabelle.

"You're safe, and you're home." Corabelle deliberately keeps her voice even and calm as instructed. She waits for the panic to clear from Marina's eyes.

"Mama! What are you doing here?" Marina sits up quickly, then sways and groans.

Catching her daughter's shoulders, Corabelle eases her down onto the bed again.

"Attempting to keep you from hurting yourself," Corabelle answers. The news she bears weighs upon her.

What will she think? What do I think? How do I tell her?

"Where's Daniel?" asks Marina.

"He was summoned before the High Council today along with Marcus and Raelyn," Corabelle explains. "They should be back tonight. Meanwhile, you're supposed to drink a lot of water and have some soup. I can get that in a moment, but let's start with the water. Will you be all right to sit up if I place a pillow behind you?"

The initial burst of energy cost Marina dearly, but eventually, Corabelle helps her to a sitting position. Next, she reaches past the amaryllis flower set on the end table to retrieve a cup of water. Carefully, Corabelle presses the cup into Marina's hands, pausing to make sure she won't drop it.

"Start with this while I go get the soup." Corabelle had heated it previously but left it on the table, having been warned her daughter might thrash when first awakened.

Since the entire dwelling could fit inside one room in any of their estates, getting the soup doesn't take her long. Upon returning to the tiny bedroom, she finds Marina resting her head back against the wall.

"Finish the water," says Corabelle, noticing the cup contains half its contents. "I want to give Raelyn a good report when she returns."

Marina's expression speaks of her fears.

"Will she return?"

"Daniel will not abandon her," says Corabelle. "Try not to worry. You need all of your strength."

"Why do I feel so exhausted?" Marina wonders. "No healing has ever affected me like this."

"Raelyn had a theory about that, but I am under strict orders to feed you before discussing it." Taking the cup from Marina's loose grasp, Corabelle brings it to her daughter's lips. "Drink up."

Predictably, Marina resists being spoon fed until a new wave of exhaustion nearly flattens her again. They forego conversation during the rest of the feeding ordeal. When the bowl finally empties and the cup is drained properly, Corabelle helps Marina back into the bed and tucks the blankets around her.

"What was Raelyn's theory?" Marina asks. Drawing her hands out from under the blankets, she grips her mother's arm feebly.

Can she handle this now?

Corabelle cannot bring herself to answer right away, so she perches on the bed and holds Marina's cool hand in her lap.

"She thinks you're pregnant." Corabelle watches the words sink in, causing shock, fear, and joy to battle across her daughter's face and manifest in her tightened grip.

Marina nods numbly as tears flow down her face.

"Are you happy?" Corabelle asks, forcing a tentative smile.

For a time, only Marina's soft sobs can be heard.

"Yes, but I'm also terrified," Marina answers, wiping the last tears away with her free hand. "What do I tell Daniel?"

"I believe it will be hard to hide the truth in a few weeks," Corabelle notes. "Does Daniel want a child?"

"He does. We do," Marina babbles, "but how do we protect a child?"

"For now, your body is doing what it can. That is Raelyn's theory of the exhaustion following the poison," says Corabelle, letting sadness and sympathy widen the smile. Leaning over, she kisses Marina's cheek. "Beyond that, love will teach you how to make peace with the worry."

The statement cannot capture the trials, triumphs, and heartaches involved in parenting, but Corabelle supposes Marina and Daniel will figure that out in due time.

When she straightens, Corabelle notices Marina's new frown.

"I can't reach Gabriella," Marina explains. "I want to tell her the news, but something's wrong."

"You're not a Minder," Corabelle says.

"I know, but she's never failed to answer, not once since the day she established the shield around my mind," Marina explains.

Corabelle had forgotten about asking Gabriella to do that for Marina to protect her during the months following her marriage to Daniel. She always figured the Minder would drop the shield of her own accord once they got established in a neutral city.

"Will you check on her?" asks Marina.

"I'm sure she's fine," says Corabelle. "Try to rest."

"No! I have to go to her."

Marina tries to sit up, but Corabelle presses her shoulders down.

"Will you promise to sleep if I go to her?" she asks, exasperated.

Collapsing onto the pillow, Marina nods weakly.

"Then, I shall go," Corabelle says. Though convinced Marina's reaction must be unwarranted, Corabelle soon needs to confirm that Gabriella is safe for her own reasons. The adoption of Gabriella Ricci into the Castaloni house for the alliance with the Polani family was meant to be in name only but it became so much more.

As Corabelle dons her cloak to leave, her fears switch focus from one daughter to the other.

Are you safe, Gabriella?

***

West Library, Polani Estate, City of Jorash

Hearing her daughter's wails, Gabriella Polani races into the library and runs straight into a man standing near the threshold. He steadies her. As recognition sinks in, a feeling of heaviness falls over her mind followed quickly by dizziness and weakness in her knees. She loses consciousness.

A sharp odor returns Gabriella's senses in a rush.

The feeling of danger strikes almost as strongly. She's been placed in one of her favorite reading chairs. Enchanted ropes bind her arms and legs tightly.

She looks about frantically until spotting Rivan holding her daughter. Katrina's cries have subsided to snuffles and whimpers, but she stretches forth both arms, desperately reaching for Gabriella.

The servant man awkwardly juggles the toddler.

"Control her," snaps Jackson.

"Ma!" screams Katrina. Her tiny hands flex in a grasping motion.

"Let me comfort her," Gabriella pleads, blinking back stinging tears.

Katrina's frustration ramps up into a full fit.

"Kill her," Jackson orders with a dismissive wave.

"No!" Gabriella stretches forth with her Gifts but quickly encounters resistance. There must be a suppression field in place. Fear for Katrina gives Gabriella the strength to reach out and touch her daughter's mind. Fighting through severe pain caused by the suppression field, she sends her soothing thoughts.

The child's fit abates.

Rivan sags with relief.

"The field won't last, so I'll be brief," says Jackson.

"Katrina," Gabriella calls, completely ignoring Jackson. Bracing for more pain, she once again touches her daughter's mind and searches frantically. She hasn't explored the developing mind much, but little brushes and images have given her clues. This time, Gabriella works frantically, trying to unlock the latent magical Gifts within the child. "Let's play a game. Hide!"

Smiling with delight, the toddler nods vigorously and vanishes.

Rivan screams and makes a swatting motion.

Hide, Kat!

A small brown beetle zips past Gabriella's head before shooting toward the racks of books and disappearing into a tiny hole near the ceiling.

The effort of unlocking Katrina's Gifts drains a lot of Gabriella's strength, but the ropes hold her in a sitting position.

She's a Shapeshifter! Oh, Marcus, I wish you could see this.

"That was completely unnecessary," says Jackson. "Keeping her quiet would have been enough."

"Forgive me if I don't trust you," says Gabriella. Though the words are aimed at Jackson, she glares at Rivan, then blinks at Jackson. "What do you want that I probably can't give you?"

"I truly bear you no ill-will." Jackson walks casually over to Rivan and places a friendly hand upon his left shoulder.

The man cries out in surprise and pain before collapsing.

"It's a good thing I put a privacy spell in place," Jackson comments. He casually moves his shoulders like they're stiff.

"What did you do to him?" Horror sends a wave of cold dread throughout Gabriella's body.

"My Master would like a brief word with you," says Jackson. "You should be honored by the privilege."

Rivan's body slowly stands and holds out a hand toward Jackson.

Slowly, Jackson draws out a dagger and places it in Rivan's hand.

The body glides over to the chair holding Gabriella.

"First, some ground rules, dear child." The voice does not belong to the servant. It's soft but cruel. "You probably lack the mental strength to reach your beloved Marcus or anybody else until the field fades, which will be soon, but hear these promises. Right now, I only require your death, but I have seeded your house with spies. If you think a word about my servant's involvement, I will kill your daughter and your husband. Do you understand these promises?"

"Who are you?" Gabriella asks. "Why must I die?"

"I have many names." The figure of Rivan shrugs and tosses the dagger from hand to hand. "Some call me the Outcast, though that is largely unfair. I prefer to be called the Dark Man. It's much more mysterious. Don't you think?"

At a gesture from Jackson, the enchanted ropes fall away, but Gabriella remains seated.

"Your sickening devotion to my enemy would be enough to make me want to kill you." Almost casually, the Dark Man places his left hand upon her shoulder.

Gabriella's entire body goes numb, but she's also frozen in place, unable to move or breathe.

The Dark man slips the dagger into her left side

She feels only a dull ache and a wave of weariness.

"See how merciful I am?" asks the Dark Man. Twisting the blade, he removes it, then lowers his voice to a whisper. "This is not about pain. It's about achieving goals. When you die, I will be one step closer to conquering this world, so thank you." Taking hold of her right hand, the Dark Man moves it over the wound. "If you hold that, you may last a few minutes longer. Say your farewells, but remember my promises."

Marcus! I'm so sorry. We have a son called Adam. Find him. Protect him. Katrina is a Shapeshifter. I love you.

Feeling her husband's frantic thoughts crash upon her mind, Gabriella repeats her message about Adam before silently begging Marcus to stay with her until the end.

Chapter 16:
Victory

Home of Daniel and Marina, City of Outreach
Five months after Gabriella's murder
(Christa's twins are about six years old)

Marina can't stop staring at the newborn, trying to memorize every feature: soft lips, delicate nose, round cheeks rosy from screaming, tiny ears, fuzzy damp hair. The baby's brilliant blue eyes cannot be seen because she has them clenched shut against the world. Her entire head nestles between Marina's cupped hands. The left one feels the full weight and warmth of the infant's head. The damaged right one senses only a little added heat.

So tiny.

A few babies had been brought to the clinic in Temperance, but never this young. Before that, Marina's previous experience with babies came decades before when her little brother, Gabriel, joined the world. She'd been too young to remember much of Jackson's early days.

A familiar ache moves through her chest.

I miss you, Gabriella. We should be sharing this moment as sisters.

Though not blood relatives, hardly a day passed without some communication between them, thanks to Gabriella's Minder abilities. The adoption had given Marina the sister she'd never had growing up. As a teenager, Jackson kept to himself, and the age gap between Marina and Gabriel gave their relationship a very different dynamic.

"You're thinking about her again," Daniel comments from the doorway.

"It's hard not to," Marina replies, still watching the baby.

If I hurt this much after more than five months, what must it be like for Marcus?

Crossing the room, Daniel leans down and kisses her lightly.

"I know," he whispers, sitting on the bed next to her. "I still don't like seeing you sad."

"Poor Marcus. Poor Katrina. Poor Adam, wherever he is," Marina laments.

The thought of Katrina Polani having to grow up without her mother makes Marina tighten her hold on the baby.

Daniel's expression turns troubled.

"What is it?" Marina asks.

Daniel shakes his head.

"I don't know," he admits. "A strange feeling, like a fading dream. Seekers don't usually feel uncertain about finding something, so not being able to help Marcus find his son is difficult. I feel like I should know where to find him, but something's blocking my abilities."

A somber mood lingers until a noise from the baby captures their attention.

"May I hold her?" asks Daniel.

"As long as you don't wake her," Marina answers. "She's just nodded off."

Making a low noise of agreement, Daniel scoops up the baby and tucks her against his chest. Her entire body fits along his forearm with her head resting upon his upper arm.

"How can one tiny being be that loud?" Marina wonders. Catching sight of a mischievous smile, she quickly adds, "Don't you dare answer that question."

Picking up her right hand, Daniel brushes a few kisses along her wrist, where she can feel them. Then, he aligns their forearms, intertwines their fingers, and clutches her hand close to his heart.

"I was only going to say she's beautiful, like her mother," says Daniel. The tilt of his head directs the soft words to the infant.

"I suppose I'll let that answer pass," says Marina.

Grinning at her, Daniel adds, "And opinionated."

Marina tries to pull her hand free, but Daniel chuckles and tightens his grip. His gaze shifts from amused to tender.

"And perfect," he finishes.

She knocks their clasped hands into his chest.

"I'm a mess and you know it," says Marina.

"Perfection goes deeper than messy hair," he notes. "Even wildly messy hair."

She grunts and nudges him again.

"Fetch me a brush," Marina orders.

The legion present for the labor and delivery had gotten Marina cleansed and put into fresh clothes, but Daniel had chased them off several hours ago. Marina had not given her hair a thought since the previous morning.

"As you wish," he says.

A brush floats up from the end table and dutifully awaits near her head. Daniel doesn't often use his Seeker abilities so casually. He hardly uses this Gift at all since he cannot always control it.

"Shall I do the honors?" he asks.

"Please." Marina holds out her arms to receive the baby.

After completing the handoff, Daniel changes position so he can reach her hair. Taking hold of a small section, he gently works the brush through, dealing with the tangles one at a time. He's become quite skilled at the task.

Marina shifts to give him more room, which he gladly takes. Before he can continue righting her messy hair, she leans back against his chest. He tucks his arms around her waist and pulls her closer, careful not to jostle the baby.

"It's really hard to brush hair like this," says Daniel, resting his head against hers. "That's not a complaint."

"If you stay close enough it doesn't matter," Marina replies, turning her head toward his.

As their lips meet, another baby noise startles them.

Marina sits up.

They bump heads as their attention fixes on their daughter.

After one more plaintive noise, the baby goes still again.

"I'll take that as orders to get back to work." Daniel continues working the brush through Marina's tangled hair, fixing it in small sections.

Marina closes her eyes to savor the peaceful moment. She idly wonders how many times Daniel has brushed her hair. It became a tradition for them in the early days of their marriage when her right hand still needed time to heal.

"Would you like something to eat?" Daniel inquires. "Raelyn left a stew, Tielle and Gabriel brought some bread, and I think your mother had a twelve-course meal prepared in Jorash. She conjured it right into place across the table, counters, chairs, and part of the couch. We're not likely to starve in the next few days, and they each promised to return tomorrow with more offerings."

"Stew sounds good," says Marina, leaning back against him once more. "But we must have an important discussion first."

"What could be more important than food?" Daniel inquires with mock ignorance. "Though I am quite comfortable."

"Our daughter needs a name, since she decided to come early," says Marina. "We were going to argue the point next week, and nothing picked before now seems to fit."

She briefly wonders how Christa came up with Dina and Devin for her twins. She can hardly believe they're about six years old now. *Will our daughter grow up so quickly?*

"What about Gabriella?" Daniel suggests. "It'd be a good way to honor her."

Marina shakes her head.

"I agree, but I can't," she says. "Besides, my brother would probably think it's for him. That would not be good for his ego."

"We could call her Marina. I kind of like that name."

Daniel's teasing tone tells her it's not a serious suggestion.

"This house only needs one Marina."

"Agreed." He stiffens. "You weren't thinking Corabelle, right? It's a lovely name, but—"

Her laughter cuts him off.

"You're safe from that, my love," Marina assures him. The thought of calling her mother's name repeatedly for the next sixteen years has no appeal. "Having namesakes is far less common for Saroth. We're more apt to choose a name based on fit and meaning. What names do you like?"

"I like a lot of names. Sarah, Elizabeth, Jane, Kylie," says Daniel. "None of them feel right for her."

Marina stares at their slumbering daughter as each name floats across her ears and agrees with Daniel's conclusion. They have prayed for this moment a long time. As her father predicted, life married to an Arkonai man involves a daily struggle even in a neutral city. Many times, their efforts to bring about peace seem doomed to failure.

She is our victory.

"Victoria," Marina whispers. Her heart swells with love for this child. "Vic."

"It's beautiful," says Daniel. "I like the long version. Should we give her a second name?"

Marina shrugs, still rolling the first name around in her mind.

"Let's add Amaryllis," Daniel suggests.

"Why do you say that?" Marina asks. Instinctively, she looks at the amaryllis flower sitting near the bed. Having at least one present has been another steady point in every place they've called home. The current sample features six deep red flowers with white centers.

"You love them, and I love you," says Daniel. He holds her closer. "They fit her. Red and white brought together perfectly. She's a child of two magic lines, neither Arkonai nor Saroth. Something new. Something wonderful."

Bending her knees, Marina turns the baby around and props her against the makeshift ramp so they can see her.

Victoria Amaryllis Saveron.

They don't confirm the name aloud. They just accept it.

After a few quiet moments, Daniel gets up and leaves the bedroom. He returns shortly with a large bowl of stew and a loaf of bread bigger than Vic.

Marina trades him the baby for the food. The stew smells delicious. Breaking off a chunk of bread, Marina dips it in to soak up some liquid and takes a large bite, sending a cascade of crumbs down her front. A sharp, bitter taste hits her. Wincing, she manages to chew and swallow.

"She added ground kayala peppers to this," Marina says, frowning at her husband. She brushes crumbs onto the floor to be dealt with later. "You knew, didn't you?"

"She said it would help you heal quickly," says Daniel. "I wasn't going to argue with her."

"It might." Marina turns her frown toward the tainted stew. "It also tastes like rancid meat mixed with dirt."

"If you finish it, I'll bring you something your mother brought," he promises. "I think I saw something with mangos that looked interesting."

"I'm going to need a lot of water."

Taking the hint, Daniel disappears into the main room and returns with two cups of water. Since he can't hold both cups and the baby, he has the spare cup hover next to him. Setting down the one in his hand, Daniel grips the floating cup.

"I'm here when you're ready."

Setting the bread aside, Marina picks up the spoon, holds her nose, and shovels some stew into her mouth. Trying not to taste anything, she swallows without chewing. Releasing her nose to breathe causes her to gag, but pinching her nose again helps control the reflex. She continues consuming the stew this way until it's gone. A few chunks of vegetables almost get stuck, but the two cups of water help her keep the meal down. The feeding trial ends in time for Vic to demand her next meal.

"I can't help you with this part," Daniel says, placing the baby back into her arms. "But I can go prep the better food while you're busy."

Watching the baby feed, Marina gains a better understanding of her own mother. Until now, the looks consisting of love, disappointment, disapproval, and terror had not made much sense.

Gabriella's murder remains a mystery because of powerful magic, but it reminds Marina how dangerous the world has become.

Can I protect her?

The answer brings Marina heartache. Since her early teen years, she has trusted the One with every part of her life. Still, the idea of being helpless to anticipate every hard thing her daughter will face, hurts. If she's honest, she cannot even prevent the child from making mistakes.

What choices will you make, Vic. Who will you become?

Every part of Marina hopes her daughter will have a life filled with peace and joy, but reality stands against the idea. She may be a victory for them, but her existence threatens many ignorant beliefs. Those who hold such beliefs have never been shy about sharing them or acting upon them. In a way, her road will be harder than anything Marina or Daniel have encountered. As a child of two magic races, the harsh reality will be that neither one claims her, no matter which Gifts she manifests.

Enjoy the moment. The One will sort the future. Marina imagines the words with Gabriella's voice. A clear image of her sister's face appears, wearing that wise, teasing expression that characterized much about her.

"I will try," Marina whispers to the memory, "but you are proof that I don't always like the future."

Chapter 17:
Shadow Needs You

Home of Daniel and Marina, City of Outreach
Eight months after Victoria's birth
(Christa's twins are almost seven years old)
"Vic! I almost stepped on you," cries Marina. "Don't eat that."

"Eat what?" Daniel wanders into the main room from the bedroom. He tugs the fresh shirt down into place.

"Daniel, come get your daughter before I spill boiling water on her," says Marina. "And see what she put in her mouth."

The baby sits behind Marina's legs happily chewing something.

Dropping to hands and knees, Daniel charges toward Victoria at a swift crawl. A high-pitched, delighted squeal erupts followed quickly by many giggles.

Shooting him an exasperated look, Marina snuffs out the cooking fire with her Saroth magic and carefully sets the large pot down on the stove. In a practiced move, she drapes the towel over her right shoulder.

"I love it when you do that with fire," he comments, ducking low to come face-to-face with Victoria. "Lighting it is even more impressive."

"It's less impressive than you think," says Marina. "What are you doing?"

"Investigating as ordered." Daniel freezes a second then jerks his head left then right then up, changing his facial expressions. Next, he opens and closes his jaw several times.

The baby giggles again and mimics the motion of his jaw,

revealing a slimy blue mass. Drool spills onto her chin.

Marina laughs too.

"Get up, you ridiculous man."

"Mamas are so impatient," Daniel says to Victoria. Picking her up, he rises and turns her to face Marina. "Nothing to worry about. It's only a blueberry." To prove the point, he sticks a finger in the baby's mouth, scoops out the blue goo, and presents it for inspection.

Victoria kicks her feet and bounces her whole body, whining at the loss of the treat.

"We haven't had blueberries for three days," says Marina. "Where did she get it?"

"They sit out on the bushes for months," Daniel points out, sticking his finger back into Victoria's mouth so she can finish the fruit.

Shaking her head, Marina removes the towel from her shoulder and tosses it at him.

"Go over there and play," she orders. "You can use the towel to clean her face while I get the evening meal onto the table."

"What is it?" Daniel asks with teasing good cheer. He knows the meal will be leftover vegetable soup and boiled potatoes because they've had the same thing the last few nights.

"Don't start." Marina's tone is even but her eyes shine with tears.

Picking up on the mood shift, Victoria melts into sobs and lunges for Marina.

Next instant, Daniel's arms are empty, and he's watching his women weep. Reacting on instinct, he wraps them in a tight hug.

Marina gives a half-hearted effort to push him away before resting her head on his shoulder, leaving enough room for Victoria.

"What is it?" This version of the question has a very different meaning, but Daniel hastens on, not wishing to dwell on the question that prompted the trouble. "What's wrong? How can I help?"

He thinks while he waits for the sobs to fade to sniffles. The days and months since Victoria's birth have passed in a blur. Daniel's teaching duties in Bastion nearly doubled when Huntmaster Winston retired. Though he's happy to come home every day, it's often not until late afternoon or evening. Huntmaster Ivan's recent promotion should help, but his training period could take another three months.

Marina's had a lot of help from Raelyn, Tielle Toscano, and Huntsman Callen's wife. The first two take turns watching Victoria whenever a business meeting absolutely cannot be put off, and Lady Ireena visits often with young Tellen.

"I feel like I'm failing," Marina whispers, "and I have only my stupid pride to blame."

"You're not failing," Daniel assures her, kissing the top of her head.

"Then why are we about to eat the same meal for the third day in a row when we could hire a cook to prepare a feast every day?" Marina's gorgeous eyes beg him to understand her. "I grew up with dozens of servants. Tielle's volunteered for the transfer. Several others have too. Why can't I accept the idea of a servant?"

"We don't have a cook because I'd overeat, be bad at my job, and wind up dead," says Daniel.

Despite her frustration, Marina laughs. When a smile forms on her lips, Daniel leans down and holds it in place with a kiss.

Victoria screeches, making them both wince and look at her.

"Young lady, I question your sense of timing." Daniel directs an exaggerated frown at their daughter.

Babbling something nonsensical, Victoria grips a chunk of Marina's hair and stuffs it into her mouth.

"We should probably feed her," says Marina.

"Why? I'd say she has excellent taste in hair." Raising his eyebrows, Daniel leans back so he can get the full effect of Marina's reaction.

Groaning, she pulls out of the embrace long enough to remove her hair from Victoria's mouth.

"Sometimes, I question if there's a serious bone in your body," says Marina.

"Who needs to be serious when in love?" Impulsively, Daniel picks Marina up and spins her around in a circle.

Her surprised cry mingles with laughter from Victoria.

The towel falls off his shoulder, but he catches it with his magical Gifts and directs it to the table.

"Put me down," says Marina.

He does so but stays in her personal space, resting his head upon hers.

"I want to hold you forever," he declares.

"I'd like that too, but we—"

A loud rumbling from his stomach cuts her off.

"Have responsibilities," Marina finishes. "Now, release me so I can feed you and this squirmy one. You can hold me later."

Acquiescing, Daniel takes Victoria and tries to stay out of the way while Marina drains the water from the pot holding the potatoes and puts the soup into bowls. The meal that follows is a messy affair as they take turns feeding Victoria small bits of vegetables. Daniel marvels at how much he's come to enjoy meals without much meat. Saroth cuisine is not completely devoid of meat, but it heavily favors grains and vegetables.

Guess meat is less appealing with Shapeshifters running about.

Daniel steers the mealtime conversation to lighter topics like some antics from his young students. He spends much of his time training Seeker apprentices to discover and use various aspects of their abilities. However, Huntmaster Winston had been responsible for the first-year apprentices, including Devin Lekros. The mention of Shadow makes Marina thoughtful, but Daniel doesn't pry for fear of prompting more tears.

"Poor Christa," says Marina. "I can't imagine having to leave Vic in the care of others. I think that's part of my fear of having servants. I think I'll miss something."

"There are supervised visits home every week," Daniel says, refraining from commenting on her fears.

"It's not the same," Marina argues. "You're home every day, and you still miss a lot of Vic's accomplishments."

"I can't not work," Daniel comments, catching the hint. They've had this discussion many times. "The Guild's—"

"Short on Seekers," Marina finishes, getting up to clear the table. "I know."

Feeling the mood shift to melancholy, Daniel holds Victoria and searches his mind for a solution to their problems. He struggles because even defining the issue can be difficult. It's not about the money. The Castaloni holdings give them more than enough to live on. It's about the principle. If he left the Hunting Guild, he wouldn't know what to do. The old dream about setting up his own Seeker business might work, but he honestly doesn't know if he is brave enough to try. Arkonai culture revolves around men being able to provide for and protect their families. The feeling of failure that plagued Marina earlier falls upon him hard.

For months, he's been working on a cabin in the woods on the Karnok Mountains. He'd wanted to surprise Marina with a quiet retreat, but now that it's almost complete, he's not sure if she will enjoy it.

"You're awfully quiet." Marina places a hand on his shoulder. "And she's out cold. Go lay her down, then you can hold me while we argue about why we make things harder for ourselves."

Daniel cherishes the short walk to the bedroom to deposit Victoria into the crib. When he returns to the main room, Marina meets him with a passionate kiss.

"I think I'll go away and return again," he murmurs when they break to breathe.

"I've missed you," says Marina.

"I've only been gone a minute," says Daniel, settling his arms around his wife. "But this is nice."

As he leans in for another kiss, Marina places a finger on his lips.

"I forgot to tell you. Gabriel and Tielle got engaged."

"Good for them," Daniel says, kissing her finger. "I'm guessing they want to steal you away to plan the wedding. Was that what you wanted to argue about?"

"Yes. No," says Marina, thoroughly confusing him. "Yes, they asked me to help plan, but the wedding won't be for a few years. They want to have a house built near Jorash first. And no, that was not the argument I had in mind, though we should talk about moving sometime. Vic will eventually need her own space."

Before Daniel can inquire about the intended argument, several frantic knocks shake their door.

"Master Daniel!" The voice is muffled but urgent. "Please help!"

Releasing Marina, Daniel hurries to open the door.

"Annie!" Marina pulls their friend inside. "You're trembling. Here, sit down." Grabbing a kitchen chair and moving it closer, Marina eases the Bereft woman onto it.

After checking to make sure they have no more visitors, Daniel closes the door and studies the servant. He's only ever seen her at Shadow Oaks. Wild strands of graying-red hair stick out from her once neat braids. Dirt lines the bottom of her long cloak. The strain and fatigue on her face speak of a long journey.

Daniel kneels before the woman and takes her hand while Marina fetches a glass of water.

"What brings you to Outreach?" Daniel asks.

Annie's gaze sharpens.

"Oh, Master Daniel. Lady Christa needs ya, she does," says Annie Kerns. "Shadow's gone."

"Gone where, Annie?" Marina asks, folding the water glass into the servant's free hand.

"He disappeared, milady," Annie declares. "Huntmaster Ivan

and Huntmaster Norval took some of the wee ones into Bleakwood Forest for a short camping trip. A storm came up. Several wee ones scattered. They found the others, but not young Master Shadow."

Located west of Bastion and southeast of Cardeth, Bleakwood Forest features many hiking trails and training outposts. Trips there are quite common for huntsmen. The closest traveler's portal Daniel can take will be to the village of Coolwater Creek, assuming the camping trip happened on the forest's east side. If he can borrow a horse in the village, he could make it in a matter of hours. Walking will add a few days.

"When did this happen?" Daniel demands. "Why wasn't I told?"

"I'm tellin' ya, Master Daniel," says Annie. "Master Jordan sent word to Lady Christa, knowing she'd send fer yer help."

"But he can't appear weak," says Marina.

"Aye," Annie confirms. She squeezes the cup of water hard. "'Tis the way of it. Will ye help?"

"He'll help," says Marina, holding a hand out to him.

Taking Marina's hand and dropping Annie's, Daniel rises.

"Take the Teleportation scroll. It's in the end table by the bed," says Marina.

"But that's for emergencies," Daniel protests.

"Shadow needs you," Marina replies. "That's reason enough."

Agreeing, Daniel dashes to the bedroom and finds the scroll exactly as described. He pauses by Victoria's crib to peek in. Marina's arms encircle his waist.

"Take this." Marina places a soft black mask into Daniel's hands.

Spinning around, Daniel faces her.

"It belongs to Shadow," Marina explains. "Annie said it'll help you find him. I'll see she gets some rest and send her back to tell Christa you'll find him. Don't make me a liar."

"I won't," Daniel promises.

After a quick kiss, Daniel concentrates on the child's mask and lets his Seeker Gifts absorb everything known about the boy's presence. Next, he opens the Teleportation scroll and bids the spell to take him to Devin. Depending on how much magic interference he encounters, Daniel should arrive close to his target. Even applied this way, Teleportation scrolls tend to be accurate, but experience has taught him to expect anything.

Chapter 18:
Next Volunteer

Library Catacombs, City of Temperance
Four days after Shadow's disappearance
(Christa's twins are almost seven years old)

Sounds of a scuffle carry Jackson's attention up from the ancient text on Darkland creatures. It's become his favorite way to break from normal studies. His master promised to teach him how to unlock Darkland portals someday. He needs to learn everything he can about what kinds of beings he could unleash upon the world. They are only a means to an end. Once they accomplish the goal of destroying the existing governments, he'll need a way to control them or send them back through the portals.

Do not be concerned. I have instructed Barsi to deliver the next volunteer.

"I can't work here. There's not enough room," Jackson protests. "The creatures will destroy the private retreat I've established."

Did you bring the Transportation scroll?

"I can get one, why?" Jackson inquires.

Take the girl to the ruins, if you desire a more comfortable locale.

"She could die," says Jackson. "Those scrolls aren't guaranteed to support life. I designed them to go through the Darklands."

Death is almost a foregone conclusion but let us present her options anyway to be fair. Be a good host and greet her.

Jackson obediently moves to the room's center as Barsi enters, followed by two men dragging a woman. Ropes bind the captive's hands

116

in front of her body, and a black hood covers her head. The grim expressions and rumpled clothes of her escorts speak of a tumultuous journey thus far.

"Hello, Raelyn," says Jackson.

"Jackson?" The prisoner stops moving. Her voice contains disbelief and fear along with confusion and hope. "Where am I? Why am I here?"

I would like to speak with her. Do we have a body at the Earth Temple Ruins?

Yes, but it's two days old.

Jackson receives a mental impression of deep disgust.

That will not do, but Barsi does not seem to care much for his current help. Draw him to you, then send the other three to the combat arena. It is best suited to containing them while we discuss the future. We must take better care of our stock.

"Where's the money?" asks Barsi.

"On the desk," Jackson says, gesturing to the four boxes he stacked as a makeshift desk.

What if the girl dies?

Then we shall count that as her decision.

"A pleasure as always," says Barsi. As he draws even with Jackson, he gives a small nod, indicating awareness of the new plan to leave with his men.

Not bothering with a reply, Jackson uses a Transportation scroll to move Raelyn and the two men to the combat arena in the Earth Temple Ruins.

I must join with you when we get there, but it will be brief.

Jackson opens a tear in the Veil and conjures himself into the ruins. As he appears in the combat arena, he experiences the thrilling rush of energy as his master's spirit temporarily inhabits his body. He spares a glance around, admiring the sheer size of this arena. His personal combat arena in Fort Medron can house three, maybe four prisoners along its walls with several paces between them. This place could hold dozens.

Three bodies litter the combat arena sand near the north wall. Two draw ragged breaths, but the third has his neck bent at a strange angle.

Move me to the living man. The other body is damaged. We will turn him later.

Jackson kneels by the breathing man and touches his shoulder.

A sharp pain pierces his hand as the transfer takes place. The man cries out, but his pain ends quickly. Used to the pain, Jackson barely registers the discomfort.

By this time, Raelyn has pulled off the hood. Pain lines her face. ***Get her chained before she fully heals that broken arm.***

Raelyn resists until Jackson grips her left arm and squeezes. She screams and tears pour down her face.

"Cooperate and you will have the chance to heal your wounds," says the Dark Man.

Jackson leads her over to a set of chains fixed into the stone wall and waits.

"Heal the bone," instructs the Dark Man. "Then, my servant will bind you properly."

Closing her eyes, Raelyn bows her head and uses her Healing Gifts. Slowly, her face relaxes.

With the Master's silent approval, Jackson cuts away the crude ropes and fixes Raelyn's hands to wrist manacles positioned above her head.

"Best bind her waist and feet before we begin," says the Dark Man. "She seems high-strung."

"We thought you changed," Raelyn comments, watching Jackson sadly. "It's going to break Marina's heart to know we were wrong."

Jackson refrains from commenting until completing his tasks.

"A broken heart will be the least of her worries soon," he says.

"Why are you doing this?" Raelyn's gaze moves from Jackson to his master. "Who is this … spirit you obey?"

"We have more important questions to discuss, but you may address me as the Dark Man or the Outcast, as you like."

A shiver runs through Raelyn at the Dark Man's second name.

"I see from your reaction you've heard of me," says the Dark Man. Working through the dead man, he straightens some of Raelyn's blond hair. "Good. Then perhaps we can skip over some threats and needless posturing."

"I belong to the One," says Raelyn with a trembling voice. She closes her eyes to avoid looking at him. "You cannot claim my soul."

"I'm not interested in your soul, only your body," the Dark Man assures her. "You will help my servant accomplish his next task. The question up for discussion is how you will render that aid."

Raelyn's eyes fly open. She flips her attention from the Master to

Jackson and back again. She starts to shake her head, but the Dark Man catches her chin and holds it fast.

"I won't help you hurt her," Raelyn declares.

Despite the words, Jackson reads the fear written across every part of her face.

"You haven't even heard the role options," says the Dark Man, releasing Raelyn's chin. "Option one, you contact Marina Castaloni-Saveron and have her meet you along with her daughter at a location my servant chooses. That is the pleasant option."

Anger replaces some of Raelyn's fear. She shakes her head.

"The unpleasant option is much more painful and traumatic for both of you," notes the Dark Man. He pauses for dramatic effect. "We kill you, trap your soul in the Darklands, and bind your essence to a scroll or a soulstone. You then become part of the team that will do the same to Marina."

"If you can accomplish what you claim, why do you need me?" Raelyn wonders.

"The message will sound more natural if it comes from you," Jackson explains.

"I have no doubt Marina would willingly trade her life for yours, but not her daughter's life," says the Dark Man. "We would be forced to retrieve the child separately, which would involve killing the person left to mind her. I haven't the patience for the complication."

Raelyn's pale skin turns even whiter. She draws shallow breaths.

"Calm yourself," orders the Dark Man. "Perhaps it would help if I described the rewards for choosing the pleasant option."

"I. Can't. Help you." The young woman's chest heaves with the force of suppressed sobs.

"Calm her before she passes out," the Dark Man orders Jackson.

Conjuring a cup of water, Jackson offers Raelyn a drink. When the cup empties, he places it back into the Veil.

After almost a minute of silence, Raelyn's breathing returns to normal.

"Since I know your heart is set on the One and money alone will not sway you, I will describe your rewards in terms you'll understand," explains the Dark Man. "In exchange for good service, I will not have servants burn your clinic down again, nor will I have them murder your parents. I also promise not to harm your brother or his family. You too shall walk away with your life intact, and because I am generous, I will add a modest sum for you to start anew anywhere you wish."

"I would think those 'promises' fall under 'complications you haven't the patience for,'" says Raelyn. She holds the chains to take the pressure off her wrists and leans back against the stone walls.

"Perspective is a wonderful thing, child," replies the Dark Man. "When it comes to plans, I prefer to dispense with unnecessary aggravation. When it comes to promises, I relish seeing them fulfilled."

Do what you can to persuade her. Small kindnesses may yield good results.

"I do not require an answer immediately," says the Dark Man. "Spend the evening thinking. Pray, if you must, but do so quietly. You can give my servant an answer on the morrow."

Done with the body, the Master lets the physical form collapse next to the other body in the arena.

Deal with the corpses first. The demonstration may help the young lady make a wise decision.

Accepting the order, Jackson conjures a blank scroll and speaks the spell to bind one of the bodies to the magic within. One corpse vanishes. He repeats the process again until the other body disappears. During the second binding ceremony, Jackson watches Raelyn to see if it has any impact. Judging by her rigid posture and disgusted expression, Jackson concludes it's having some effect upon her, though he cannot guess which way the reaction will push her.

Do you have a soulstone?

I keep some in my study.

We may have need of it but try to persuade her with words.

"Would you like to sit down?" Jackson asks.

Opening the Veil, he sends the scroll into one of his storage areas. Before the tear mends, he admires the large collection of similar scrolls stored in this vault. Pride warms him when he considers the hundreds of vaults he's started filling. Some only contain one scroll, as he tries to keep them separated by what type of soulless body is bound in place.

Raelyn's eyes say much about her disgust, confusion, and despair, but she nods in answer to his question.

Reaching up, Jackson changes the way the chains work. Instead of two separate manacles attaching to one long chain, the wrist bindings are held together by a very short section of new chain. One part of the main chain connects to a ring on the other section, letting it slide up to the top ring, which lengthens the prisoner's leash considerably. Next, he detaches the foot bindings from the wall chains. Finally, he releases the chain around her waist and lowers her to the ground.

"Thank you," Raelyn whispers. Scooting back and tucking her legs close, she manages to rest her bound hands upon her knees. Once settled, she studies Jackson. "Why are you helping the Outcast?"

I would also like to hear the answer to the question.

"I was promised power and a position of importance," Jackson answers with a shrug. "That was how it started anyway. Now, I serve my master to learn." The conviction he feels surprises him. "I can do things no Conjurer has done for hundreds of years, maybe thousands."

The Healer does not need to know the extent of your power. If she helps us, I would like to let her live.

Not since the last Great War was an army of undead set upon Aeris.

Soon, my servant, but focus on the current task. Gain the Healer's cooperation. We must obtain the bracers.

"What does the Outcast want with your sister?" asks Raelyn.

How much should I tell her?

Partial truths might help. Promise that everything will end happily for your dear sister and her quaint family once Daniel retrieves what we desire.

"Marina is a means to control Daniel Saveron," Jackson answers. "I need him to find something for me."

"Ask him," says Raelyn. Her hands grip the chains tightly. "Daniel's a good man. Offer my life if you must, but don't involve Marina and Victoria. Please. Don't you feel anything for them? They're your family."

Kneel by her. Plead with her. Be her friend.

Obeying the suggestions, Jackson crouches before the captive.

"My master does not make idle threats," he says. "Marina's fate is sealed. Yours is not. You can't stop us, only inconvenience us. Save yourself and your family."

More tears gather in her eyes.

Now, leave her to ponder the situation.

Chapter 19: Provisions

Marina's Office, Castaloni Shipping Headquarters, City of Outreach
Four days after Shadow's disappearance
(Christa's twins are almost seven years old)

Marina rises as an assistant ushers Mika Forester into her office. Conscious of every move, she steps gracefully from behind the desk and moves to greet her guest. Things go well until the last step wherein she trips on the long, green dress and falls toward the man. Crying out, she throws out her hands for balance.

Catching her hands, the man steadies her.

"Lady Marina, it's wonderful to see you too." His dark eyes twinkle with amusement.

"Please, Master Forester, we're alone, and you've known me as long as I've been alive." Marina forces her shoulders to relax and refrains from reclaiming her hands. "I have enough people bowing whenever I enter a room. I need friends and allies, not sycophants."

"Well, we must go on record today, but for the first few minutes, I accept the role of friend and ally." Chuckling, Mika pulls her into a warm embrace then backs up and admires her dress. The friendly air shifts into solemn sadness. "Antonio would be proud of what you've become, Mari. I'm sorry to be the one standing here in his place."

"Don't be. He would have had it no other way. He trusted you completely." When Marina lets her hands fall to her sides, the voluminous sleeves fall and engulf her hands. She frowns.

Ridiculous fashion. How does one get anything done in this contraption?

The beautiful gown features tiny gold vines and flowers from the upper sleeves and bust down to the waist. To balance the gaudy main portions, the bulk of the skirt and lower sleeves consist of rich, green silk that flows around her arms and legs like gentle wind. Of her formal dresses, she favors this one best because it is Daniel's favorite color. Like her, he prefers simple dresses, though their reasons differ. She likes everyday dresses for practicality's sake, and he likes them because they are approachable.

You can't embrace sequins without pain. The thought replicates Daniel's teasing tone and inflection perfectly.

Turning away to hide the expression, Marina retreats to her desk.

"Let's finish the business discussion quickly so we can visit more," says Marina. "I can have Tielle bring Vic by. She's grown since you saw her a month ago."

"That is motivation enough for me," says Mika. "Do you have a privacy scroll and a recorder scroll ready?"

"As requested," Marina confirms, picking up both scrolls and handing them to the counselor and purser.

Mika wastes no time activating the scrolls and giving the introductory speech, which includes the parties present, the date, and the purpose for the meeting. He next launches into a lengthy legal speech explaining the conditions those mentioned in the will need to meet and some acceptable forms of delegation if they want to retain rights without such burdensome responsibility. Finally, Mika begins the series of important questions.

"If something should happen to you, such that you could no longer perform the duties as head of house and chief decisionmaker for Castaloni holdings, who would you like to effectively run the house, lands, and businesses in your stead?"

Having been given the list of questions and their anticipated order, Marina doesn't hesitate. Her answer's longer than most would be under similar circumstances due to the unprecedented situation of her life.

"My heir is my daughter, Victoria Amaryllis Saveron, but she will not come of age for many years. As such, she needs a guardian, caretaker, and sponsor or manager. My first nominee for caretaker and guardian is my husband, Daniel Saveron. However, as an Arkonai, he has the right to refuse the position of manager if he desires. In that case, my second nominee for any remaining role available is my younger brother, Gabriel Castaloni, and his wife. He has no wife currently but has recently become engaged to Tielle Toscano."

"Do you have a third nominee?" asks Mika.

Marina winces at the implication. A third becomes necessary if Daniel refuses and Gabriel's unavailable.

Daniel, are you safe?

It's a dumb question, but one she's lost count of over the years. This isn't his first multi-day mission, only the first in a few weeks. At least in the past she had the comfort of knowing Marcus could protect him and could rely on Gabriella for regular updates on their well-being. This time, he's alone.

The One is with him.

Marina forces her thoughts back on track.

"My third nominee is my mother, Corabelle Castaloni. My fourth is Marcus Polani." She stops speaking when Mika gives her a curious look and pauses the recording.

"You should list your brother Jackson somewhere," Mika advises. "I know that is the last thing you want, but it will raise a lot of questions if a non-family member gets nominated before him."

Marina stares at Mika and double checks that the recorder remains paused. The privacy spell will magically enforce the conversation's confidentiality, but she's not certain she should burden her father's closest friend with the truth.

"Marcus is family. Besides, the sponsor or manager will control large portions of my daughter's life," Marina says.

And that's not happening, ever.

"If my husband and I are unable to fulfill our parental roles, I want to ensure she's loved and protected. Marcus has a daughter a few years older than Victoria, one who has lost her mother, my adopted sister. My hope is they'll be good friends soon."

"Was Gabriella older than Jackson?" Mika asks, sitting up straighter.

"I believe so," Marina answers, picking up on his excitement.

"Wonderful. We can continue." Mika releases the recorder spell to continue. "Please list any and all remaining nominees."

"Fifth would be the Tariku League. In the absence of previous choices, I submit the fate of my daughter's guardianship to the High Council." A painful truth stabs Marina. Her people may reject Victoria because of Daniel's bloodline. She shuts her eyes to move the pain enough to speak. "If they refuse to decide the matter or cannot reach a decision, I appeal to the High Council of the Arkonai Hunting Guild.

Should it come to that, please see that Raelyn Cordova and Lady Christa Lekros are present when they discuss the matter."

Mika stops the recording again.

"Your mother has told me there is strife between you and Jackson. Off the record, would you tell me about it? Has he hurt you?" Mika gestures toward her right hand, a question in his eyes.

"He's not responsible for this," Marina says, studying her damaged hand. "Not directly anyway."

"Then why not include him?" Mika presses.

Marina's mind pulls up the memories surrounding the River's Edge tragedy where Jackson involved innocent people in a personal war against her. He'd unleashed a disease against villagers, then offered her the antidote in exchange for her birthright and her Destroyer powers. He'd even succeeded in claiming most of her Gifts, but her father never acknowledged the destruction of her Keeper's pendant, the item that would allow her to safely pass through Caramore's magical barrier. A guest could be granted access through a portal room in Dominance or Jorash, but a citizen without a Keeper's pendant is an exile.

"He poisoned our father." Marina lets the statement linger until it sinks past the shock it causes in Mika. Despite the many years, tears burn her eyes. She blinks to hold them in, but their essence comes out in her voice. "I can forgive my brother for every wrong done to me personally, but to this day, I struggle with that one. Worse, there's an ancient law—"

"The Unforgivable Crimes Act," Mika finishes. "Something meant to protect now denies you justice." A far-off expression comes to him. "I've been meaning to petition for striking down that law."

"If it were only me, I might say something anyway," says Marina. "But Mother and Gabriel don't deserve to suffer for Jackson's deeds."

"They are already suffering, but I see your point," says Mika. "Nevertheless, let us include Jackson ahead of Gabriel as tradition dictates, but add in some additional safeguards."

Marina had hoped to avoid this, but Mika's right. Not including Jackson will raise too many questions.

Tradition or not, if Jackson is added, it'll be to the end of the list. He is not coming near my daughter.

She hasn't forbidden him from seeing Vic, but she also hasn't extended any invitations for him to visit either. A fierce wave of protectiveness spreads through her for Vic and the businesses.

I just have to make inheriting intolerable to Jackson.

Taking a deep breath, Marina describes the many provisions, stipulations, conditions, and limitations set to kick in if Jackson ever inherits the holdings.

If he wants money, he gets no control. If he wants the title, he forfeits the profits.

As they finish the modifications to the will, something thumps into the door.

Marina prepares to ignore the noise, but it sounds again.

"Go ahead and answer it. Our business is already on hold."

"Who is it?" Marina calls.

"Sorry, Lady Marina. Vic got away. It won't happen again." The harried voice belongs to Tielle.

Yes, it will. She's a very fast crawler.

"Come on in." Marina looks to her guest. "I think Master Mika would enjoy a short visit."

The delight on his face confirms it.

The door swings open, letting Vic zip inside.

Abandoning his chair, Mika races to intercept Vic before she can reach the bookshelves.

Marina watches Tielle hover near the threshold. The woman's plain beige dress bears several colorful smudges. A larger, wet spot shows a futile effort to remove something.

"Go get some rest," Marina orders.

"I can—"

"I know you can handle her, Tielle. You've proven as much the entire day. Sit down. Get something to eat. Check back in an hour."

"Thank you, Lady Marina. Are you certain?"

"I am." Marina smiles as her brother's future wife shuts the door. They'll eventually have to work on informal addresses, but she supposes the circumstances warrant formality.

The door swings open.

"She never finished her evening meal," says Tielle. "Would you like me to bring it to you?"

"Thank you. You can put it on my desk." Marina moves a container of ink, the spent privacy scroll, and the recorder scroll off to the side to make room.

One by one, three small bowls appear as Tielle conjures them. The first and second bowls hold orange and green paste respectively and come with tiny wooden spoons. The last has three blueberries in it. Marina waves once everything's in place, and Tielle exits again.

"What delights does the evening meal hold today?" Mika inquires. He holds Vic over the desk so she can view the spread.

Marina studies the contents.

"Mashed carrots and peas. I think." Her last two words undermine the confidence in her tone. "And blueberries."

"Bubba!" Vic points urgently to the third bowl.

"May I give her one?"

Nodding, Marina holds the bowl up so the counselor can select a ripe berry.

"I should make you start with carrots, but I'm afraid your formal robes would be the worse for it."

"Dark robes hide many sins … and stains," Mika says, picking up a blueberry. "My grandchildren have proven this many times."

"How many do you have now?" Marina vaguely recalls hearing of two grandchildren, but her information is woefully out of date.

Vic's eyes track the berry carefully. She opens her mouth.

"Three. With a fourth on the way," Mika reports.

"Bubba!" Vic says, face scrunching to launch into a fit.

Just before the storm can break, Mika pops the blueberry into Vic's mouth.

They spend the next half-hour feeding Vic. Mika's skillful work results in only a few splotches of orange or green goo landing on important scrolls. At first, Marina worries if a cleaning scroll will work on enchanted documents, but eventually, she sits back and enjoys watching the normally stoic counselor entertain her daughter.

When Vic finally settles down to nap in Mika's arms, they return to the original business.

"This next question will be hard for you," Mika warns before letting the recording scroll resume. "What is the company succession if your husband and daughter are no longer available to accept the honor?"

"It follows almost the same succession as before but with my brother, Jackson Castaloni, in the front of the line," says Marina, keeping her gaze upon her slumbering daughter. "After him and any heirs he produces comes Gabriel Castaloni and heirs, Marcus Polani and heirs, and finally my mother, Corabelle. If our line is completely spent, the Tariku League can search for heirs among other branches of my father's family. If none can be found, the managers may purchase controlling interest and leave the holdings altogether."

Marina knows she'll be far beyond caring if Jackson ever inherits the holdings, for it would mean both she and her daughter are dead. Still, she must protect the holdings from Jackson any way she can. If he inherits, it will be in name only. If he tries to change anything significant, the businesses gain the option to go public with profits from the sales benefiting charities that promote healing, disaster relief, or bettering relations between the Arkonai and the Saroth.

"What would you like to do with your personal wealth if you die before your husband and daughter?" asks Mika.

"It can be held for my husband and daughter to use as necessary," Marina answers, knowing with absolute certainty Daniel will refuse most of it. "But if Daniel doesn't want it and Vic is provided for, you can give it to my brother, Gabriel."

The conversation continues across many similar lines until they generate a thorough will for Marina. She includes a provision for Daniel to have continued access to the charity accounts her father set up for her just before his death. By the time Mika deactivates the recorder scroll, Marina wants nothing more than to crawl into bed and sleep. She amends her wish when Mika circles her desk and places Vic in her arms.

"I know that was difficult, but hopefully, it will never be necessary," says Mika. He places a hand on her shoulder. "You're doing fine, Mari. The businesses are holding their own, and your daughter is flourishing. But don't be afraid to step back if you want to concentrate on this little one for a few years. The house council will not be pleased, but I can handle them. Think about it."

Chapter 20:
Discovery

Daniel's Camp, Bleakwood Forest
Same day (Four days after Shadow's disappearance)
(Christa's twins are almost seven years old)

As Daniel feeds the campfire fresh sticks, he lets his thoughts wander. Frustrating as this hunt has been, he has missed being in the woods and hearing the insects and night creatures go about their business. He had also forgotten the wonders of game cooked over an open flame. When selecting his evening meal, he'd almost killed a squirrel instead of a rabbit. His Seeker Gifts wouldn't allow him to accidentally kill a Shapeshifter, but he couldn't bring himself to finish the kill, not with squirrel being one of Gabriel's forms.

I may never eat squirrel again.

In certain forests that might be a problem, but this close to the plains, Daniel can easily find other small creatures for food or forego meat and survive on berries and plants instead. His knowledge of edible plants is not as extensive as Marina's because his Seeker studies did not cover several years studying healing arts at the Alamon Temple, but he can find enough to survive.

This would be more fun with Marina and Victoria.

Though Victoria will not appreciate camping for a few years, Daniel eagerly anticipates teaching her to live off the land. Memories of escorting Marina from the village of River's Edge up to Aridel fill his mind. They had taken a traveler's portal from River's Edge to Cardeth before hiking across the Northlands to their destination.

Does she know the trip took longer than it should have?

129

At first, the desire to talk sense into Marina ruled his choice of route, but by the end, he merely wanted to stay with her.

I loved her then.

Are you done being sappy?

"Good evening, Marcus," Daniel greets. "To what do I owe the pleasure of your company?"

Your wife is worried. Have you found the boy yet?

"I haven't found him yet, and how do you know my wife is worried? Did you speak with her?"

I don't have to speak with her to know she's worried, but we did speak last night. I promised Gabriella I would check on Marina regularly. Worried people have a different feel to them than others. Marcus's thoughts still carry the weight of his grief.

Truly not knowing how to comfort him, Daniel throws another few sticks into the fire. His collection should last throughout the evening if he's careful about rationing the bigger logs.

This would be much easier with Marina.

Find the boy so you can go home to her.

"Do all Saroth have the ability to control fire or is it a Destroyer Gift?" Daniel wonders.

That one has more to do with bloodlines than magic schools, but as with any Gift, some are blessed to possess it and others are not. I do not have that ability, nor does my sister, but my parents and my brother do. Of my five cousins, three have it and two do not. Why do you wish to know?

"I'm realizing how much I don't know about the other schools of magic," says Daniel. "I've spent my life learning everything about Seeker arts. Never had a need to know about the others, but I'm curious to know what Gifts Victoria will manifest."

When did you know you would be a Seeker?

"I'm not sure," says Daniel. "My parents sent me to a training school in Aridel when I was six, but I can recall finding things well before that. I think I've always known. What about you? When did you discover you were a Minder?"

Most Minder Gifts are harder to detect. As with most of our abilities, our Spontaneous Phase is far less visible than other schools. We don't accidentally release bolts of lightning, conjure random objects, or shapeshift with abrupt changes of emotion.

"Has Katrina discovered any more forms?" Daniel asks the question softly, knowing that the first shift happened the night of

Gabriella's murder. He balances the dark thought by recalling Marina's tale of her brother's first shapeshifting adventure. He'd taken squirrel form to avoid a bath.

Not to my knowledge, and the beetle may not even be one of her forms once she gains some control. This phase is characterized by great power and little predictability.

Daniel sits up straighter.

"Say that again," he orders.

Marcus dutifully repeats his last thought.

"Great power. Little predictability." Daniel quickly rises. "Marcus, that's it! That's what's happening."

You think the boy is in Spontaneous Phase.

"We call it Discovery, but yes," says Daniel. "Every time I've followed my Seeker senses close to him, he vanishes, forcing me to start again. I've crossed this forest a hundred times in the last two days."

What Gifts could he have that would let him vanish?"

"He's a Seeker." Chuckling, Daniel shakes his head, not sure how the truth escaped him this long. The light moment passes. "Why doesn't he sense me?"

Perhaps he does. You said he doesn't vanish until you're close.

"Why would he avoid me?" Daniel wonders. "He should be able to tell—"

Daniel cuts himself off as Marcus's next question reaches him.

Are you the only one searching for the boy?

"Apparently not."

Small signs click together in Daniel's mind. He had dismissed the subtle evidences of the others passing through because Bleakwood Forest hosts many training missions year-round. The last mystery resolves for Daniel.

"The training field," he murmurs. Smothering the fire, Daniel quickly packs up his camp and draws a short sword from the Veil. He explains for Marcus's benefit. "The Guild uses this forest to train huntsmen. There's a magical null field around the forest to keep training accidents from wiping out villages."

That might prevent the child from teleporting to safety, but why would he avoid you?

"He's being hunted by someone like me," says Daniel.

Do you have a change of clothes?

"Why would I need to change?" Daniel asks, pausing his camp

breakdown chores.

If the boy fears huntsmen, search as someone else.

Opening a small hole in the Veil, Daniel stores his packed belongings and picks up his sword.

"I see your point, but the only clothes I can access right now are more of the same." Daniel gestures to his plain brown pants, beige shirt, and dark brown vest.

At least remove the vest or forego the cowl. That might be enough of a difference.

Accepting the advice, Daniel removes the hood, closes his eyes, and turns in a slow circle, searching for the twinge that would confirm he is on the boy's trail.

Try not to teleport very close to him.

Daniel nods and makes a slight adjustment. He doesn't bother explaining the difficulties in enacting the suggestion. Properly applied, Seeker Gifts allow him to teleport directly to his target under certain circumstances. However, if his senses aren't aligned well, he could teleport miles beyond his target.

Must you carry a sword? You'll scare the boy.

"I won't have time to access a weapon," Daniel explains. He hesitates before making the first jump. With his current energy levels, he can do two or three teleporting jumps before needing to rest a few hours.

Call him by name as you arrive. His given name. It's possible the others do not know it or wouldn't bother using the name.

Finishing his internal adjustments, Daniel relaxes and lets his Seeker Gifts teleport him toward the boy's location.

"Devin!" Daniel calls, taking Marcus's advice.

As before, Daniel gets a very strong sense of the boy and then nothing.

"He's gone again." Daniel grips his sword tightly and concentrates on detecting the new direction.

Keep trying.

An arrow flies toward his face. Without even thinking, Daniel whips his sword up into the arrow, knocking it into a tree. Three more arrows converge on him.

There's no time to dodge.

He teleports toward his target again.

This time, he lands on his knees, feeling like he sprinted the entire distance.

"Devin!" Daniel knows he should get up, but instinct keeps him kneeling. "I'm not with the Brotherhood. I'm here to help. I know your mother. She's my friend."

"What is her name?"

The question comes from Daniel's left, but he holds his position.

"Her name is Christa," Daniel answers. Unprompted, he continues, knowing the boy will press for more proof before trusting him. "She was born and raised in Aridel. Her family name before marriage was Arrington. She had an uncle who was Supreme Huntmaster before your father."

"What is your name?" asks the boy.

"My name is Daniel."

Something relaxes in the boy's spirit, and he emerges from some bushes behind Daniel.

"Will you take me home?"

Turning slowly to avoid frightening the child, Daniel looks toward the voice.

The boy stands tall wearing dark clothes and a black cloth mask. The combination of bright moonlight and tall trees creates many shadows that let the boy blend in perfectly.

Before Daniel can answer the question, an arrow flies at the boy.

"Down!" Daniel orders.

The arrow pierces the bush where Shadow had been hiding.

Racing over to the boy, Daniel stands guard above him, but he doesn't like their position. It's too exposed.

Move toward the large tree to your left, then draw a bow. I can help.

"Move toward that tree over there. Stay low," Daniel instructs. Dropping his sword, he calls his short bow from the Veil, repositions to cover the child, and squeezes his eyes shut.

Fifteen degrees. Forty paces.

Relying on countless hours of practice, Daniel pictures the target in his mind, puts an arrow into place and fires. A scream reports success, but he has no chance to appreciate it. Reaching into the Veil again, Daniel nocks a new arrow. They had discovered long ago that his rate of fire increased drawing arrows from the Veil rather than a conventional quiver.

Sixty-two degrees. Thirty-nine paces. Then eighty-six degrees and closing fast.

Daniel deals with the second attacker same as the first.

The third roars a challenge as he charges.

Wishing he had a sword, Daniel braces. Normally, he'd get out of the way, but that would leave Shadow exposed.

You can open your eyes now.

Daniel does so before scanning his surroundings.

New ground. New trees.

The other ground had been softer and the trees there had been broader and older. This area has more space between trees.

"What—"

Look down.

Following the direction, Daniel spots Shadow curled onto his side, sleeping soundly.

"Looks like you saved us," Daniel says. Crouching, he puts his hand on the boy's shoulder. "My turn."

The null field prevents him from teleporting beyond Bleakwood Forest, but he jumps them to the forest's edge. Since technically Annie holds Daniel's contract and she's in Coolwater Creek, they exit the forest on the southeast side. Picking up the exhausted child, Daniel teleports them as far as he can toward the village, then begins the long trek. The jump saves him a few days of travel time, but he lacks the energy to reach the village by teleporting.

"Tell Christa, Annie, and Marina I found him," says Daniel.

What about Jordan and the High Council?

"They can wait for my official report. No sense in revealing your involvement," Daniel explains. "We're still not officially cleared to work together, but thank you, Marcus. I don't think I could have done that alone."

Will you go home tonight?

"I can't." The two small words hurt. "The Council needs to know of the attacks. Shadow could still be in danger. Tell Marina I love her."

You know I hate playing personal messenger, but fine, just this once.

"Give Victoria the same message."

Go home. The contract will be fulfilled when you return the boy to Annie. She can escort him to Bastion. The High Council won't see you until tomorrow anyway. Walk them to the portal if you must, or see them settled and go home. You have no valid excuse to avoid your family.

Marcus cuts off the flow of thoughts, but not before Daniel

detects sadness again. He wishes things could be different for his friend. He doesn't know if he could do what Marcus does in raising a daughter without her mother.

You do what you must, but also, cherish what you have.

"All right, I will. Thank you, but don't tell Marina. I want to surprise her."

The thought of seeing his wife and daughter in a few hours gives Daniel new strength for his long march to Coolwater Creek.

Chapter 21:
Hostages

Home of Daniel and Marina, City of Outreach
Earlier that same day (Four days after Shadow's disappearance)
(Christa's twins are almost seven years old)

Jackson doesn't typically wear a cowl in the middle of warm, beautiful days, but it suits his current errand. The hood prevents him from seeing Barsi, but his master assures him of the assassin's presence.

No games until we reach the temple. I don't understand your obsession, but I will tolerate it for now as long as it doesn't interfere with the plan.

After knocking on the door to Marina's ridiculously small house, Jackson crosses his arms and waits.

Why does she live in this hovel? Is Daniel gone? I don't want to deal with him right now.

I will help him with his errand so that he arrives tonight. You still have a few hours.

"Jack! What are you doing here?"

"Dear sister," he replies pleasantly. "Are you going to invite me in?"

"Answer the question first," says Marina.

He answers with a firm shove that pushes the door back into her, forcing his sister to retreat a step. Jackson steps forward and holds the door while Barsi enters behind him.

For a second, shock freezes Marina in place.

The delay gives Jackson a chance to use the privacy scroll.

Their eyes meet and reach the same conclusion.

136

She whirls and takes two steps toward the bedroom.

By then, Barsi has reached her and used a scroll that induces sleep.

Marina collapses.

Struck by the similarities to the night Gabriella died, Jackson steps over Marina on his way to the single bedroom. Once again, he's appalled by the size and rustic nature of this dwelling. His sister grew up the same as he did in homes that functioned like villages. One could easily fit a hundred houses this size inside their Jorash estate.

She could be living in the Outreach estate on the outskirts if she so desired. Mother would not deny her that privilege. She could even buy a new estate in the heart of the city.

Ruminate later. Grab the child and move Marina quickly. She will awaken soon.

Stopping in the doorway, Jackson immediately spots the crib in the far left corner, three paces away. For her part, the child clings to the crib spokes with her right hand and blinks curiously at him. Drool slips down her chin as she gnaws on her left fist.

Spotting a rag on the end table near some flowers, Jackson picks it up and cleans the baby's face. Next, he drops the rag into the crib, picks up the child, and cradles her with his left arm. Her deep blue eyes capture him. They're exactly like his sister's eyes. Impulsively, he traces one of the baby's cheeks with a finger. The odd sensation feels good. If he didn't know her father was Arkonai and her very existence could destroy the world, he might even like the girl.

She babbles something unintelligible at him.

"Hello, little one, I am your Uncle Jack," he says. "You don't know me because your mother never introduced us. How terribly thoughtless of her."

Marina is awake now. Demand her cooperation.

Turning the baby around so that she is seated across his arm facing outward, Jackson enters the main room.

"Jack! What are you doing?" Marina sounds breathless.

Barsi has moved her to a sturdy wooden chair. He stands directly behind the chair, out of her line of sight.

Jackson cannot see her hands, but the awkward set to her shoulders tells him they're likely bound behind her.

"I'm visiting my niece, whom I've never even laid eyes upon," Jackson says with mock indignation.

With the child in hand, your sister will obey almost any

command. Use the Teleportation scroll.

"Who is the man behind me?" asks Marina.

"So many questions," Jackson comments. He moves to a position a few feet in front of his sister, so she can view the baby in his arms. "This might be our longest conversation in years. Do you find that sad?"

No games here! This must be finished at the secondary site.

This won't take long. Jackson assures his master.

"Children are such delicate creatures," says Jackson. "I once heard of a Bereft boy who tumbled out of his mother's arms all the way to the hard ground. He was lucky a traveler had a Healing scroll handy to preserve his life. Do you know why I tell you this story?"

He has the pleasure of watching horror sweep over Marina's expression.

"Beg for her life." Jackson props the baby up so Marina gets a better view. "Look at her. So soft. So delicate."

"What do you want from me, Jack?" Marina asks. "Money? Power? I have nothing for you. Even if I resigned, the house—"

"I want what's mine!" Jackson's grip on the child tightens, causing her to fuss. "What should have always been mine!"

"Don't hold her so tightly!" Marina pleads, leaning forward as far as the bonds will let her. Frustrated tears shine from her eyes. "You'll hurt her."

"If you value her life, you will follow my instructions very carefully," says Jackson. "Will you do that for me?"

Marina's expression wavers between fear and weariness, eventually settling on weariness.

"Where did we go wrong?" Her question comes out soft and reflective. Her gaze turns distant. "We were friends once."

Move her now!

"It doesn't matter," Jackson declares. "We need to leave."

"No."

"No?" Jackson echoes.

"I'm not making this easy for you," says Marina.

Turning the baby around so she can face him, Jackson holds her up.

"I don't think your mother cares much for you, little one." He tosses the child up into the air and lets her plummet toward the ground. Just before her body would hit the floor, Jackson conjures a cushion beneath her.

Marina screams.

The baby giggles.

Tears stream down Marina's face.

The look of terror and desperation fills Jackson with joy.

The child crawls off the cushion and moves toward her mother.

A piercing pain flashes through Jackson's head, stealing his satisfaction.

Enough childish games. Give Marina the baby and bring them to the temple.

With a small nod, Jackson gives Barsi permission to cut Marina's bonds.

As soon as she's free, Marina rushes to her daughter and cradles her close. More tears fall, but Jackson suspects some of them carry her relief.

Opening a small tear in the Veil, Jackson puts away the cushion and retrieves a Teleportation scroll. He holds the scroll out to his sister.

"Take this and go to the destination," he instructs.

"Let me leave Vic." Marina's kneeling position enhances the plea.

"You'd abandon your only child?"

"It's better than whatever you have planned for her," Marina answers evenly. "Daniel will know what to do. He can take care of her."

Knowing the answer, Jackson appeals to his master for a decision.

Bring the child.

"I would like to grant your request, but my master would like Victoria to take the journey with us." Jackson watches Marina while the state of helplessness sinks in.

Barsi helps her stand.

The plain light blue dress with white sleeves makes Marina look like a Bereft villager. A brown belt circles her waist, accentuating the Arkonai influences in her clothing choices. A woman in her position ought to be dressed in robes that equal her elevated station.

"Why?" Marina hugs the child closer and gazes upon the baby's face. "What are we to your master?"

Tell her I will speak with her once she arrives at the temple.

"He will explain when you get there," Jackson promises, still holding the scroll out to her. "Put on a travel cloak. You will need it."

Marina only stares at the proffered scroll.

Threaten the child or tell Marina about the Healer.

139

Jackson senses his master's impatience.

Barsi picks up a royal blue cloak and drapes it around Marina's shoulders. He throws the hood up over her head and hands her a white wrap for the baby.

"You will take this scroll and follow it, or my friend will drop your child. He's not a Conjurer. There will be no cushion," says Jackson.

"What happened to you, Jack?" Marina asks, accepting the wrap from Barsi and bundling the child.

"We can catch up properly later, but your Healer friend would probably appreciate it if we hurried."

Marina blinks to absorb the painful revelation.

"What did you do to Raelyn?"

"There is still time to save her if you heed my master."

Holding the baby with one arm, Marina reaches out and tentatively touches the Teleportation scroll. She doesn't have to read it. The enchanted parchment releases the appropriate spell as her fingers brush the scroll.

Marina and the baby vanish.

"Wait for Daniel," says Jackson. "He should arrive in a few hours. A sleep scroll should work, but he's Arkonai. Their magic works differently, so don't be surprised if it fails. Make it clear he only gets to see Marina and the child if he obeys, and you should have no more problems with him."

"I know my business," says Barsi.

"I know you know," Jackson snaps, "but it bears repeating. We need him alive with his magical abilities intact."

Without waiting for a response, Jackson opens a large hole in the Veil and steps through, conjuring himself to the same place he sent Marina and Victoria.

As he rejoins the natural world at the Earth Temple Ruins, Jackson feels his master's spirit join his own. The place feels more like a forest than an ancient temple. Tall tree trunks blend in with the crumbling pillars. The afternoon sunlight shines down through the canopy like beams of holy light.

The Teleportation scroll had delivered Marina about ten paces from Jackson's entry point. She stands with her back to him.

The scroll was not calibrated properly. Take her to the arena.

"Marina," Jackson calls. "This way."

The baby sobs.

Marina turns. Everything from her expression to the set of her hands around the baby shouts her fears. She leans down and whispers to the child, rocking her until the cries subside.

Go. She will follow. Mention her friend again.

"Raelyn's waiting."

As predicted, the words pull Marina along the narrow path.

"Where are we going?" Marina wonders.

"To your friend." Jackson decides it's easier to humor her with small talk than listen to her prattle the entire way.

"Why is she here? Why are *we* here? None of this makes sense."

"She is here for you," says Jackson. "You are here for Daniel."

Sharp head pain assails him.

Do not mention the huntsman. Her love for him is greater than for the girl. We must control her first.

"What do you want with Daniel?"

Something in Marina's voice alerts Jackson to the fact that she's stopped walking.

Halting his own progress, he faces her.

"I promise answers await inside."

"Tell me right now. Do you intend to kill him?"

Answer her honestly but briefly. Get her to concentrate on the Healer.

Jackson shakes his head.

"My master has a task for him to complete."

Marina doesn't move. Her gaze drops to her daughter.

"We are hostages."

Jackson nods.

"As is Raelyn, but you don't get to bargain for her until we're inside."

Though not as quickly as before, the words have the desired effect. Marina falls into line as Jackson finds the main entrance to the ruins and descends into the depths toward the arena. Designed similarly to many early forts and fortresses, the Earth Temple's combat arena doubles as a dungeon. As they enter hallways too dark to see, Jackson reaches for the Saroth Gift for fire and lights the torches lining the path.

As they descend, the air becomes cooler, making Jackson grateful for the dark, heavy cloak.

Each step closer to the arena increases Jackson's anticipation. As they reach the sandy area, his fingers twitch with nervous energy. Throwing his arms out wide, Jackson lights the torches spaced throughout the circular room in succession. He starts with those closest to him and moves the fire toward those placed around Raelyn and another prisoner. The second captive wears beige pants and a dark brown vest as befits the boring nature of huntsmen. Jackson had considered lighting the torches simultaneously, but the successive option has a more dramatic effect.

Noticing the light's still too inadequate for a proper presentation, Jackson conjures six scrolls containing strong energy orbs and activates them. Sensing each other, the orbs spread out and move up until the cavernous arena is evenly lit.

Marina draws a sharp breath and stumbles forward, drawn inexorably toward her friend.

Jackson knows exactly what she's seeing, for the scene likely hasn't changed since he arranged it this morning.

Raelyn hangs from chains fixed to the north wall, arms spread wide, head bent forward, and eyes staring blankly at the sand.

Well done. Seal the entrance. We have your sister's full attention. Transfer me, and I will finish this phase.

Reaching the far wall, Marina touches the Healer's face, then withdraws her hand quickly.

"What's wrong with her?"

"She's dead," Jackson replies.

Chapter 22:
Moral Decisions

Combat Arena, Lower Level of the Earth Temple Ruins
Same day (Four days after Shadow's disappearance)
(Christa's twins are almost seven years old)

"She's not dead." Marina feels the truth in the words as she murmurs the denial. Somewhere, there's a faint, broken, but unmistakable spark of life within Raelyn. Grasping the slippery ends of her courage, Marina reaches out again and rests her left hand on Raelyn's cheek. The flesh feels cold and hard like a stone covered in frost. Her fingers tingle from contact with dark energy, but she forces herself to maintain the touch.

When you asked me to train you all those years ago, I wanted to say no.

Marina's vision blurs with fresh, hot tears.

Actually, I think I did say no, but you knew I didn't mean it and pressed harder, until I gave you the answer you wanted. I should have stuck with no for your own good. How many times have you faced danger because of me or my choices?

"You are correct." The male voice sounds simultaneously cultured, ancient, bored, and dangerous. "As is my servant in saying she is dead. Would you like to know how to save her?"

"Yes!" Marina cannot keep the desperation out of her voice. Wrapping both arms around Vic, she pivots to face the speaker.

A chill lances through her.

The voice comes from the other prisoner. He no longer hangs next to Raelyn. Instead, he stands beside Jackson, posture straight, and chin held high to receive her scrutiny. The spaces that should hold his eyes shine with supernatural red light.

"You may address me as the Dark Man. Forgive the flair, but if

143

I fail to project light, only the whites show. That terrifies people and impedes our ability to converse. Would you prefer green light instead of red?" He makes the appropriate change.

She's heard the title before but lacks time to dwell on it.

"What must I do to save her?" The question saps much of Marina's remaining composure.

Picking up on her mood, Vic starts crying.

"First, you should turn that baby over to Jackson for safekeeping," says the spirit inside the corpse. "In your distressed state, you're likely to suffocate her."

Jack takes two steps toward her.

Marina retreats two steps. The move brings her close to Raelyn. The Healer's blank expression strikes her as hard as any physical blow. She backs up yet another step, bumping into the stone wall next to her friend. Instinctively, Marina hunches her shoulders and spins away from the dark spirit.

"Please don't take her!" Marina loses track of the times she voices the plea.

"It was not a suggestion," says the Dark Man. "But I assure you, we're very early in negotiations. She'll be quite safe for now."

A wave of weariness sweeps over Marina. She falls toward the wall, barely having the sense to brace herself with her left arm and push hard enough to turn her body as her legs collapse. Nevertheless, her right arm stays firmly around her daughter. She lands facing her friend.

Vic stops crying.

The resulting silence frightens Marina.

Crouching before her, Jack gently removes the baby from Marina's arms.

The oppressive state vanishes.

Marina's aching arms feel cold and empty without the baby's familiar form. She stares hard at her daughter, willing Vic to cry or give another sign of life.

"She's only sleeping," the Dark Man says. "I figured our discussion would be more peaceful this way. You have some important decisions to make, and I would like your undivided attention."

"I'll pay better attention when I know she's safe," Marina admits, still staring at Vic.

"Very well." The spirit snaps his fingers at Jack. "Conjure the baby's crib and set her down."

Jack obeys. Vic's crib appears, disturbing some sand as it lands next to him. He wastes no time laying the baby in place.

"Now, be a gentleman and help your sister up."

When Jack reaches down, Marina grips his hands hard.

"Jack, who is he? Why are you helping him?"

"I believe I already introduced myself. I am the Dark Man. I'm going to excuse the lapse because of your trying day, but I expect better from you very soon."

By the end of the Dark Man's speech, Marina's on her feet but still holding Jack's hands. She finally remembers where she read the name before.

Knowing this might be the last moment to redeem her brother, Marina speaks low and fast.

"Your master is the Outcast. He stands against everything right and good. Turn away from him, Jack. Serve the One."

"Do not mention that name in my presence!" The dark spirit's eyes flip from green back to red.

Father, save us.

Gripping her right elbow, Jack leads Marina to his master. He drops her arm and steps away once they come within two paces of the figure.

For the first time, Marina notices the earth-tone clothes. The fitted vest reminds her of Daniel. Her heart lurches.

"Is the huntsman dead?" She cannot detect a spark of life, but the dark spirit's presence could be masking it.

"Unfortunately, yes," replies the Dark Man. "This crude means of communication is the very problem I'm hoping you'll help me rectify."

While she waits for the spirit to explain, Marina turns left to look at Raelyn then right to look at Vic's slumbering form. Upon returning her attention to the Dark Man, Marina finds him staring expectantly.

"What is your request, child?"

"Awaken Raelyn and send her away with Vic."

The Dark Man gives her an exaggerated look of confusion.

"I currently have three hostages. Why should I give away two?"

"Because you only need one," Marina replies, working hard to keep her words steady. "Jack said Raelyn was here for me and I was here for Daniel. You have me now, so you can let her go."

The Dark Man draws closer.

"What of the baby? Should I not hold her to control you and your beloved huntsman?"

"If you hurt her, my husband will die fighting you." The certainty settling in Marina's chest puts her on steadier emotional ground.

"What if I hurt you, do you expect the same reaction?" The Dark Man keeps his tone light and curious. In contrast, he steps close enough to smell the dried sweat lingering on the body.

Without looking at him, Marina counters with a question.

"What do you need him to do?"

"He's a very talented Seeker, so he's going to fetch something for me," says the Dark Man, backing out to a less threatening range. "Something powerful that will allow me more than a few fleeting moments on this terrestrial plane."

"He won't help you." A tremor reveals her statement to be more wish than fact.

"He won't know he's helping us," Jack explains. "He'll think he's saving you."

"Saving me from what?"

"An endless cycle of torment as one of the undead," the Dark Man announces cheerfully.

Horror keeps Marina silent. She turns her attention to Raelyn and stares until the ability to speak slowly returns.

"Is that what you did to her?"

"That was merely an experiment," answers the Dark Man. "One we're not quite done with. Shall we see if it worked? We'll let Jackson do the honors."

With a snap of his fingers, Jack conjures a smooth black stone and hands it to her.

The dark energy pulsing off the stone makes Marina's stomach queasy. She runs her fingers over the smooth surface.

"Hold onto that. It is a soulstone," explains the spirit. "One that currently holds your Healer friend's essence. We've already summoned one of the undead to infect her with their unique disease and then put a ward around her body to prevent wandering souls from filling the void."

Marina follows his gesture to a gash on Raelyn's left arm. She hadn't noticed before because her eyes had been drawn to the Healer's fixed expression.

"In theory, returning her soul should return her to life, which is why I claimed you were both correct," the Dark Man finishes.

"But she'll turn," Marina says, tucking the evil thing into a pocket in her cloak.

"I have a theory about that too, hence the trouble we've gone to with this elaborate presentation," says the spirit. "I believe you can save her through your Destroyer Gifts."

"My Gifts were stolen." The words hurt less than they have in the past.

The Dark Man waves the statement away like a bothersome gnat.

"Jack merely took the lightning. That's the flashy aspect everybody expects of a Destroyer. He did not know of the other piece of the Gift because *you* did not know of it at the time, but I witnessed what happened in the woods near River's Edge. You healed Gabriel."

"I can't explain that," says Marina, "but it wasn't Destroyer Gifts. That was a Healing of some sort. It shouldn't have been possible, and I was only able to do it because I had strength from Daniel."

"I believe it's a sign." The corpse's face twists into an expression mixing disgust and contempt. "The Lady of Light favors you. She gives you what you need when you need it, to a point. Thus, we come to the first major moral decision. Will you save the Healer, knowing you may not possess the strength to drive the disease off yourself later?"

"What other choice do I have?" Marina wonders.

The Dark Man glances at Jack who conjures a dagger and holds it out to her.

"You could kill her," says the spirit. "If her body expires, her liberated soul can wander the Darklands. She may even find her way to the portal leading to Kailon's current lair."

Marina shrinks away from the weapon, prompting a chuckle from the Dark Man.

"If you do nothing, she will turn and could potentially harm the little one," says the Dark Man. "You must choose."

"Will you let her live?" Marina's question is rough with grief.

The Dark Man signals Jackson who conjures a Teleportation scroll and tosses it to the sand halfway between Marina and Raelyn.

"Second moral decision," announces the Dark Man. "My plans are always flexible. There lies a means of escape for you or the Healer. I'll even allow it to be for both of you, if you desire. It's set for Midpoint. You can stay in the village or port to a major city and retreat anywhere you like. I will keep your child to get what I need from Daniel. If everything goes well, I may even return her to you someday."

"Let Raelyn take Vic with her," Marina pleads, repeating an earlier sentiment. "Daniel will come for me."

The Dark Man shakes his head.

"I require her as a backup in case you die on me. Moving souls about is always tricky business. Hence my need to practice on the Healer," explains the Dark Man. "Victoria, of course, cannot drive the disease away when her part is done, but I may be able to use the artifact Daniel acquires to preserve her life."

Marina imagines racing for Vic, then diving for the Teleportation scroll. The vision melts when she looks at her unconscious friend.

"What say you to these moral questions?" intones the Dark Man. "What shall we do with the Healer?"

"I will save her and send her away," Marina answers.

Vic, forgive me. I cannot leave you here alone.

"Predictable, but you are entitled to that option," says the spirit. "Go to her. Jackson will release her from the chains and secure one of your wrists to the wall. Do you have a preference?"

Heart pounding, Marina shakes her head.

"Regardless, he will ensure you have enough chain to reach the Healer. When you are ready, he will release her soul and give you a few moments to drive off the disease. If you succeed, the girl goes free, and we'll find a new undead volunteer to infect you before sealing your soul within the stone. If you fail, you'll probably be infected. In that case, Jackson will release the girl with his dagger."

"Who will take care of Vic?" Marina asks. "It could take Daniel hours to arrive."

"I'm sure Jackson can conjure something to keep the child alive," replies the Dark Man. "Otherwise, I'll keep her asleep to maintain the peace."

"We have the time. May I see to her needs?" Marina braces for a negative answer.

Jack and the Dark Man exchange a brief look.

Shrugging, Jack picks up the Teleportation scroll and conjures a wooden chair and an ornate folding screen in front of the crib.

The Dark Man waves, releasing the sleeping spell surrounding Vic.

She starts crying. The sound fills Marina with conflicting emotions, bringing tears to her eyes.

"The entrance is sealed. You cannot escape, but we have time to pass," says the Dark Man. "See to your needs and the child's. Jackson will provide a suitable meal for you. We can awaken your friend later."

Mention of Raelyn draws Marina's attention back to her. The skin near the wrist chains looks raw.

"Did you hear me?" The Dark Man sounds mildly amused.

"Please release her from the chains," says Marina.

"She can't feel anything," Jack points out. He looks to the spirit for approval.

"Do as you wish," says the Dark Man. He sits upon the sand, then lies down. "My time in this vessel is at an end."

Jack conjures a key and tosses it to Marina.

Catching it, she hurries to release Raelyn. She starts with the two ankle bindings, then moves to the one around the Healer's waist, before finishing with the wrists. Vic's wails provide a heartbreaking counterpoint to the struggle to free Raelyn's body. It's hard work because Marina tries to keep Raelyn propped up during the release process to avoid dislocating her shoulders. She cannot do it alone. Eventually, she calls for Jack's help, and to her surprise, he gives it.

Once Raelyn's settled safely on the ground, Marina arranges the Healer's hands across her stomach and silently prays for protection.

Then, she dashes over to Vic, picks her up, and cries with her.

I can't lose you, Vic. Not for anything. I love you too much. If I must fight every spirit in the Darklands, you will live. I promise.

Chapter 23:
Demotion

Gathering Hall, Village of Coolwater Creek
Same day (Four days after Shadow's disappearance)
(Christa's twins are almost seven years old)

Daniel spots the yellow and green tunics of two Pirok Guards standing outside the Gathering Hall. Their presence means Jordan Lekros must be close.

I didn't think Jordan ever left Bastion these days.

The guards straighten as Daniel approaches. The one closest to him opens the door for him and speaks.

"The Supreme Huntmaster is waiting."

The statement doesn't mean much to Daniel until he steps inside and finds the hall packed with huntsmen and Pirok Guards. Dozens of lanterns provide plenty of light. A hush falls over the crowd. They part to give Daniel a clear path to the front.

He spots his friend standing on a wide platform built across the front, but his attention fixes upon the woman standing beside Jordan. Thick ropes bind her wrists in front of her body and worry lines her face. The expression melts into one of pure relief.

"Master Daniel. I see ye found the lad. Thank the Lady," says Annie.

"He's safe," Daniel assures her.

"Why is my son unconscious?" Jordan demands.

"Why is Annie being restrained?" Daniel asks.

"It's protocol for letting a stranger near the Supreme Huntmaster," explains a haughty man standing on Jordan's other side.

150

Daniel recognizes the speaker as Huntmaster Mason Pine.

"She's not a stranger," Daniel protests. Angry steps carry him across the Gathering Hall to the front. "Jordan, you know her."

"You will address the Supreme Huntmaster with proper respect, or I will have you removed from this hall," says Huntmaster Pine.

"I doubt the Supreme Huntmaster would approve, since my contract's not complete and the boy's in my custody," says Daniel. His head throbs with frustration. He glares at his friend. "Release Annie immediately."

"We know only that she wears the face of one of Lady Christa's servants," explains Huntmaster Pine. "With the increasing number of Saroth wandering our lands, there's a chance she could be an imposter."

"Face-altering spells have existed for centuries," says Daniel. "They can be bought in almost any market by anybody, but I've never heard of one that could mimic a person's thoughts. Are you telling me that in this entire crowd you could not find one Seeker to scan her surface thoughts for deception?"

A flicker of guilt crosses Jordan's face.

He never thought of it. He wanted her to be an imposter.

Stretching forth with his Gifts, Daniel confirms Annie's identity.

"Take off the bindings so I can complete my contract," Daniel orders. He doesn't bother masking his disgust.

Everyone looks to the Supreme Huntmaster for a ruling.

Jordan nods.

Two Pirok Guards move to cut the ropes away. Before they reach her, the Guardian controlling the enchanted ropes bids them to unwind and return to him.

"Complete the contract." Jordan's impatience is clear.

"Have a Healer tend to her wrists," Daniel argues.

"'Tis nothing, Master Daniel," Annie says, descending from the platform. "Lady Christa can see to me needs later."

"I'm sure the lady has more important things to do," mutters Huntmaster Pine.

Annie sits on a nearby wooden bench, and Daniel places Shadow in her arms.

As her arms wrap around the boy, Daniel studies the marks.

"I'm sorry," he murmurs, meaning the words for more than the physical wounds.

"'Tis not your doing," Annie replies, hugging Shadow tightly.

"Seth, bring me my son. Ivan, take Annie home. Jonas, prepare the hunting party." Jordan's orders come out crisp and clear, but his expression remains weary.

Daniel turns to protest, but Annie stops him with a look and wakes the child.

"Mum?" asks Shadow.

"No, love, but yer da's here," answers Annie. "Wake up. I think he'd like to see ya."

The handoff runs smoothly.

A young huntsman carries Shadow over to Jordan while another helps Annie up.

"I'll take her home," Daniel offers. The extra errand will delay him an hour or two, but he will be able to personally reassure Christa of her son's safety.

"That won't be possible," says Huntmaster Pine. "First, you're going explain yourself."

"What's to explain?" asks Daniel. "I was hired to find Shadow, and I did so. You'll have my report in a day or two."

By this time, most of the crowd has exited the Gathering Hall. Only Huntmaster Pine, Jordan, two Pirok Guards, and Shadow remain. After a long embrace, Jordan sends his son off with the two guards into the back room.

"Tell me about the hunt," Jordan orders. "How did you come to possess a contract for my son?"

Daniel tries to understand the stiff set to his friend's shoulders.

"You know how," he replies.

"How long have you been in contact with my wife?"

The question shocks and amuses Daniel, but since Jordan's anger seems genuine, he controls the urge to laugh.

"I've hardly spoken to her in years," says Daniel. "Hardly anybody has since you put her away."

His statement refers to Jordan's ceremonial denial of Christa as his family, a ridiculous notion put into his head by Pine and other idiots with Resolute ideals. They claim the tradition protects loved ones from becoming tools for one's enemies. Since that time, Jordan has gone to pathetic lengths to please everybody. Daniel has even heard through Marina that they have co-hosted dinner parties with a screen between them to prevent Jordan from seeing Christa.

"Answer your Supreme Huntmaster," snaps Pine.

Daniel's jaw hurts. He tries to rein in his temper and only partially succeeds.

"Years. Decades. We met in a Discovery class when I was six. She was seven. I made fun of her hair. She punched me. We've been friends ever since." Daniel silently admits he's been a lousy friend to Christa the last few years and promises to do better. "That was a few months before I met you." He directs this statement to Jordan.

"You know what I mean. Why does she feel comfortable coming to you?" Jordan demands.

"I don't know," Daniel answers honestly. "Why don't you ask her?"

"You know I can't." Jordan rakes a hand through his sandy brown hair.

"How dare—"

"It could be she's comfortable with me because she kept in touch with Marina," says Daniel, before Huntmaster Pine can finish blustering.

Pine looks smug.

"It's as I told you, Supreme Huntmaster. The Saroth influence is dangerous. You should put a stop to this at once."

"Why does this bother you?" Daniel strains to keep the question curious instead of accusatory. He really wants to summon some ropes and a gag for Pine like he did when he first met Marina. A smile forms at the memory, but the ever-present scowl upon Huntmaster Pine's face destroys the good feelings. "Christa—"

"Lady Christa Lekros," Pine interjects.

"Lady Christa needs friends," says Daniel, still pointedly ignoring Pine. "She once saved Marina's life. The friendship is good for both of them."

"He's not referring to Marina and Christa," Jordan clarifies, looking distinctly uncomfortable. He makes a calming gesture that puts Daniel on edge.

"This is about you and the Saroth woman," Pine explains.

"What does *my wife* have to do with this?" Daniel looks from Pine to Jordan.

"I'm sorry, Daniel. I had no choice. I needed two extra votes on the restoration of Fort Faith."

Huntmaster Pine beams.

A brief silence falls.

"What did those votes cost?" Daniel's question breaks through the thickening tension.

"You're the best Seeker we have," says Jordan. "It's time you accepted contracts again."

Understanding spreads over Daniel.

"Speak plainly," he says.

"Your services as an instructor are no longer needed," Huntmaster Pine announces. "Huntmaster Mercade will see you get contracts that suit your skill level."

Part of Daniel welcomes the prospect of fulfilling Seeker contracts again, but Pine's satisfaction irritates him.

You'll be away from Marina and Victoria for long periods of time.

Daniel does not relish the coming conversation with Marina. He winces as he imagines the hurt, graceful acceptance she'll display. His heart fills with love for her. Bowing stiffly to Huntmaster Pine and Jordan, Daniel turns away.

"We have not dismissed you yet, Huntsman Seeker." Pine flings the lower rank like an arrow.

Daniel takes it in stride. The rank had been handed to him with the role. He only went through with the promotion and teaching position because of Christa's request and the ability to spend more time with his family. He'll miss working with the apprentices and the first-year huntsmen, but the idea of being far away from Huntmaster Pine offsets the disappointment.

Sorry, Christa. Jordan doesn't want my help.

"This could be temporary." Jordan's words give Daniel time to face them again.

"Let's make it permanent." Daniel opens a tear in the Veil and removes the small silver coin he earned with his first Guild contract.

Before he can return the coin and quit the Guild forever, somebody pounds on the Gathering Hall doors. They fly open with a bang.

"Courier's here with a message for Huntsman Daniel," says the Pirok Guard who'd let him into the building.

A young man dressed in comfortable clothes strides in and presents Daniel with a scroll.

The message fills Daniel's head as soon as his fingers fall upon the enchanted paper.

Come home alone. Your family needs you.

"Excuse me. I must go." Dropping the scroll, Daniel sprints past the courier.

Pine starts to protest but Jordan stops him.

"Let him go." His grim tone says he probably knew the scroll's contents.

"Are we going to help him?" Pine asks.

"No. We cannot help him," answers Jordan. "That's all I was told."

Daniel flies out of the Gathering Hall, missing the rest of their discussion. Coolwater Creek's portal only connects to Bastion, so he switches there to one that will take him to Outreach.

By the time he arrives home, sweat covers him head to toe. He pauses long enough to draw a sword from the Veil. Since his favorite short sword still lies somewhere in Bleakwood Forest, he chooses a greatsword that belonged to his father. A desire to pray goes no further than a desperate cry for help. A sense of caution kicks in before he can charge straight through the door.

"Marcus, what am I facing?" Daniel's Gifts would allow him to detect presences, but he's too upset to use them.

Four men.

"Marina? Victoria?"

They're not at that location, but the leader's mind feels calculating. He will have answers for you.

Will they attack as I enter?

The leader has a sleep scroll primed, so yes.

Searching his feelings, Daniel pictures the tiny bedroom. If he can connect to something familiar and specific, he can teleport there. Usually, this portion of his Gift works best with people, but it only functions at close range. Marina's not close enough to sense, but when he casts about for something to use as a focal point, the fading amaryllis flower by the bed flashes in his mind's eye. Seizing the connection, Daniel teleports. The move weakens him, but it also gives him a distinct advantage over his enemies.

The crib's gone.

Still holding the greatsword, Daniel pushes the oddity out of his mind, opens the Veil, and selects four throwing daggers coated with powerful sedatives. The recipe came from a collaboration between Raelyn and Marina, once they realized he wanted an alternative to the deadly poisons chosen by most huntsmen. Daniel hasn't attempted controlling four daggers simultaneously for ages, but the house's small size works to his advantage. Marcus helps him with the distance calculations based on the minds present in the next room.

Daniel drops the daggers until they float just above the floor. Next, he sends them toward his targets. At the last moment, he directs them upward so each dagger flies into a man's lower left leg. Two wordless cries and a loud curse follow. Daniel waits for three thumps to follow then steps out and bring his sword up to the leader's neck.

"Why are you in my home?" Daniel demands, moving to a position where he can see the man's face. "Where are my wife and daughter?"

The initial panic clears from the man's dark eyes.

"I carry a message." The man's dark hair and features tell Daniel he's probably Saroth. "Your family will be returned after you Seek something for the Master. May I show you the contract?"

"Slowly," Daniel instructs.

The Saroth man reaches into his robes and pulls out a scroll. Still holding the sword in place, Daniel grips the contract. Nothing happens.

"It's not enchanted, but I can tell you what it says."

"Speak quickly then," Daniel orders. Anger gives him the strength to hold the heavy sword steady.

The man stiffens, staggers back a step, and grips the side of his head.

Daniel lowers the sword but keeps the last throwing dagger hovering behind the man.

"The Master invites you to see his handiwork. Lay down your weapons, and you will be taken to them."

Chapter 24:
Life and Death

Southwest Slums, City of Resilience
Same day (Four days after Shadow's disappearance)
(Christa's twins are almost seven years old)
Settling his sister in for the reprieve costs Jackson Castaloni more energy than he'd expected to spend. Instead of stopping with the privacy screen and the chair as planned, he brought her a small table and summoned a full evening meal from the Jorash estate. Next, he conjured a rocking chair from nothing and provided fresh clothes and wraps for the child. He'd even retrieved a few blankets for Marina's Healer friend because he knew it would please her.

Why do I care what she thinks?

You want to impress her. You always have. No matter. You know how to recover quickly.

After checking the seal across the combat arena's entrance, Jackson travels to Resilience. He tries not to visit major Arkonai cities more than once or twice a year to avoid causing too much of a stir. Usually, he refrains from working until the darkest hours of night, but he lacks the luxury today.

Conjuring a few copper coins, Jackson moves through the poor section toward the market. The closer he gets, the more ragged people he sees. The city smell hits his senses hard as the day's heat still lingers. It's a combination of sweat, waste, and desperation. Arkonai cities always smell awful because they're too proud or stupid to use masking spells correctly, at least in the sections he frequents.

With his hood up, Jackson blends in with the Bereft villagers and adventuresome Saroth wandering the dusty streets on one errand or another. The weariness manifests in his gait, further aiding his efforts to blend in. He buys a loaf of bread from a merchant and subtly conjures more coins before returning to the intersection containing the most beggars. Wandering between the wretched people, he doles out portions of bread and coins until he finds what he's looking for.

A woman leans against a broken crate. Her coin bowl lies empty near her feet. Occasionally, a coughing fit overtakes her, shaking her entire body.

An outcast among beggars. There's always one.

The one will do, but hurry. You must finish this task and move on before it's discovered. You have other work to complete.

Leaning down, Jackson drops two coins into the woman's empty bowl, drawing her attention. Next, he places the remaining scraps of bread into her dry, cracked hands. She cries but lacks the energy to speak as Jackson siphons her lifeforce and uses it to replenish his own. The woman didn't have much life left in her, but it's enough to make Jackson feel normal.

Yet another vital lesson Master Polani failed to teach me.

His devotion to the One limits his vision and ability. You do not have that flaw. That is why you will surpass him.

Jackson moves through the poor section with new vigor, searching for the right candidates for this next part. When he spots three men huddled together, he ducks into a nearby ally and sweeps for witnesses. Once assured of privacy, he conjures a set of fine Arkonai clothes. Since he lacks the time to color his hair with kessemi roots, he selects a simple illusion scroll from his stash. He could have used a scroll with a face-altering spell, but there's no need for him to pass close inspection today.

Adapting his walk to match observations of upper crust Arkonai native to Resilience, Jackson strides out of the alley and marches toward his victims. Whereas before their gazes flitted over him with disinterest, now he commands their attention. Without acknowledging their presence, he steps by them and keeps moving at a fast clip, headed for the north entrance to the merchant zone. As he passes the next alley, someone shoves him hard. Jackson harnesses the momentum to put some distance between him and the assailants.

A snap pulls two scrolls from the Veil. Upon striking the ground behind him, they deploy the Transportation spells. He's usually not so wasteful, but he can't afford to miss one of the men.

"Give us your—"

The assailant can't even finish the threat.

By the time Jackson finishes turning around, the men are gone.

Time to see what we've caught.

In theory, he's sent the men to the combat arena currently holding Marina. If he's lucky, they'll be alive but weakened by the journey. Given past experience, at least one or two should have some life left to draw. If they all die, he'll have to choose another city and go hunting again. That would be unfortunate, but it's happened before.

Stepping through the Veil allows Jackson to enter the arena just as one man recovers his feet.

You need me.

Without further explanation, the Master's spirit joins Jackson again, giving him unnatural strength, speed, and knowledge. The Arkonai man possesses Guardian Gifts. He calls a sword and takes a defensive stance, but before he can move or think of a protection spell, Jackson slams into him with enough force to carry them to the wall next to Raelyn's prone form. The sword disappears.

The man's scream and the crunch and crumbling sound of breaking stone brings Marina around from the privacy screen. Jackson doesn't have to see her. He can sense her through his master. Thankfully, she's momentarily speechless. Seizing the advantage, Jackson chains the Guardian to the wall and presses his head hard into the wall, using the Master's power to put him into a deep sleep. It's the only way to safely hold such a man prisoner without resorting to methods that would detract from his uses.

With the danger past, Jackson feels his master's spirit leave him. He steps back to admire their collective accomplishment. The Arkonai man breathes deeply and regularly. His peaceful expression would make more sense if he was tucked safely into a bedroll and not hanging from the arena's stone walls.

There is still life to be had from one man. The other died along the way. Teach your sister this lesson before she needlessly wastes her strength trying to save him.

Jackson stretches forth with his spirit to feel the truth of his master's statements before letting his eyes confirm the words. He finds his sister already kneeling beside one of the Arkonai men.

"He'll be dead soon." Jackson waits for her to check the claim.

"What happened to him?" Marina picks up the man's hand and

holds it.

"Doesn't matter," Jackson answers. "You look weary. Let's not waste this opportunity."

Marina slowly raises her eyes to meet his. Familiar deep disapproval marks every inch of her face.

"Draw energy from him," Jackson orders, kneeling on the man's other side. "The same connection that lets you transfer part of your life to others in extreme circumstances will allow you to do so in reverse."

She won't do it. Take the energy for yourself but let her know the other man's life is hers. She may need that for the Healer.

Jackson conveys the message and draws the dying man's magical reserves into himself.

"How long?"

"How long what?" Jackson knows exactly what she means by the question, but he refuses to make the discussion easy on her. If she wants to travel the moral high road, she'll have to climb to get there. He stands and dusts himself off. Noticing the Arkonai pants, he conjures his dark cloak and swings it into place. A proper change can wait.

"How long have you practiced forbidden magic? Served the Outcast? Had any sort of regard for life?"

Contempt and anger fill him so swiftly and strongly that he cannot reply right away. However, the longer he stays silent, the more of her anger morphs into pity. He finds that worse.

"I've been studying a long time," says Jackson. "Ever since the day my great and mighty former master refused to show me the advanced Conjuring arts."

"They're forbidden for a reason." Marina arranges the man's arms in a more peaceful pose.

"Why should I let cowering fools tell me where to limit my power?" Jackson demands.

"Advanced Conjuring arts require life energy, same as any other school of magic," Marina argues. Shifting her legs to a more comfortable position, she leans back on her hands. "Safely drawing such energy without harming everything around takes decades of practice."

"Turns out it's a lot easier if you don't care who dies."

"Do you truly not care who dies?"

"Of course, I care!" The need to make her understand burns in Jackson's chest. "I'm very selective about who I draw from."

Marina's expression turns unreadable.

"Today, I killed a woman who probably wouldn't have lasted the night. She received rest. I received a magical boost. Where's the harm in that?"

She winces at the question but does not interrupt his passionate speech.

"Dozens expire every day, forgotten by every civilized society. They die in gutters, dark alleys, and sometimes in the middle of a market. The city patrols collect them and burn or bury them as tradition requires. Nobody notices or cares if one more body joins the count."

"You're right."

Jackson's ears perk up. He mentally examines the statement from every side. His heart beats faster.

Does she truly understand?

For an instant, Jackson lets himself hope he won't have to continue the quest for knowledge alone. His sister could come to her senses, follow the Master, and help them find more believers among their people.

"Deep apathy plagues every society." Marina pushes off the sand and stands. "But knowing the problem doesn't mean we give up or make it worse." She gives him another long, intense, vexingly unreadable look before retreating to the crib holding her daughter.

Curious, he follows, expecting her to pick the child up. Instead, she grips the railing and watches the baby sleep. Not understanding the appeal, Jackson watches and reluctantly admits it's relaxing.

"I used to watch you like this for hours," says Marina. "We had our own rooms, but I spent more time in yours than mine. Mother lectured about leaving you alone, but Father eventually had somebody put blankets next to your crib."

Jackson's heard the tale before, but he doesn't stop her. It's better than arguing or hearing more drivel about righting society.

"I saw the first time you conjured something, though I guess it was more of a summoning," says Marina. "I was almost asleep, but the faint movement of air brought me awake. A stuffed wolf lay beside you. Then a duck. Then half-a-dozen more stuffed animals. I was torn between running to tell our parents and staying to make sure you didn't bury yourself. I didn't get them, but they must have sensed something. That time Father yelled, but being a Conjurer, Mother understood. She spent the next two weeks sleeping beside me in your room in case you conjured something more dangerous."

"That was a very long time ago," Jackson comments. "People grow up."

Marina offers him a sad smile.

"I want that version of my brother back."

"He's gone," Jackson says flatly.

She shakes her head in denial.

"I don't think so. You've always cared more for people than you'd admit," says Marina. "There wasn't a night of Gabriel's early life that you'd let his crib stay empty. Mother had to demand you only bring him one stuffed friend per night."

"The foolish notions of a child," Jackson counters.

"When Carmen Imis lost her grandmother, hundreds of calla lilies surrounded the funeral pyre during the celebration of life ceremony. Nobody claimed credit for the deed, but I know it was you."

"I was infatuated with her," Jackson says defensively. "It meant little then. It means less now."

Releasing the crib, Marina faces Jackson.

"It means that somewhere under that cold front you project lies someone who cares very deeply. I hope you'll remember that one day."

"I'm sure you'll be there to remind me," he says, exasperated.

Marina blinks back tears.

"Your master can't abide people like me," she whispers. "No privacy spell will hold your secrets forever. Eventually, I'll remember the events of this day, and he'll have to silence me."

"We need you alive to motivate Daniel to do his part."

"I still don't think he'll help you, but I could be wrong." Marina studies her dusty hands. They're almost a matching shade of gray-white now. "Let me awaken Raelyn. If I die, you can send Mother and Gabriel my love, assuming your master hasn't turned you against them as well."

"You're not going to die!" Jackson's irritation spikes. "When placed under stress, your body will defend itself. That's why we have another prisoner ready for you to draw energy from."

Marina makes no more comments, but her body language reads stubborn.

I think she wants to die.

Remind Marina that living is in her family's best interest. If she disrupts my plan by dying, I will enslave her daughter's soul, get what I need from her husband, and destroy them both for the inconvenience.

Chapter 25:
A Different Way

Combat Arena, Lower Level of the Earth Temple Ruins
Same day (Four days after Shadow's disappearance)
(Christa's twins are almost seven years old)
The Dark Man's latest threat hardly fazes Marina, for she knows it to be no different than his original plan. While Jack traveled abroad the past hour, she has spent nearly every second deep in thought and ministering to Raelyn or Vic. Jack's sudden return soon after bodies rained down from nowhere disrupts her work, but she picks it up again while they watch Vic sleep.

Over the years of shielding her mind, Gabriella taught her many lessons, including how to think on several levels simultaneously. Strong emotions and mundane tasks allow one to create the thought equivalent of a droning noise, which can mask inner thoughts. Marina doesn't have to work hard to find strong emotions. The tasks of feeding and changing Vic bring comfort, but she still has much to fear.

On the surface, the Dark Man's deal seems straightforward: infect Marina but move her essence to a soulstone until Daniel ransoms her life with an artifact.

Why use a soulstone?

Holding her prisoner would work for a time. Even Daniel's Seeker abilities could not lead him to her instantly unless the danger became more immediate. The best Marina can figure, the soulstone and infection routine constitutes a magical timer. There hasn't been a problem with the undead for centuries because most of the Darkland portals were sealed after the last Great War. However, it would only take

163

a skilled Minder or a Conjurer to summon a spirit to finish the turning. A soulstone could preserve her essence indefinitely, but her uninhabited body would be limited to a matter of days or weeks unless surrounded by very strong magic.

The promise of waking Raelyn is a ruse, something to occupy Marina and keep her calm until Jack and his master can move their plan forward. They have no way of knowing what she will remember upon awakening. Few have returned from soulstones. The magic could completely reverse the privacy spell Jack put in place. It's safer for them to let her body perish.

The same holds true for keeping Vic alive. They need her to control Marina, but that hold is tenuous.

The Outcast cannot let her live.

Once upon a time, as a student at the Alamon Temple, Marina took breaks from her healing studies by reading historical and religious scrolls stored in the archives. Nearly everything written on the Outcast spoke of his burning hatred for children with mixed magic lines. The Redeemers, an old religious order devoted to the One and the Lady of Light, wrote a lot about the Chosen Redeemer, a powerful being who could defeat the Outcast. The prophecies were exceptionally vague and sometimes contradictory, but most insisted both magic lines would be heavily involved. Hence, the vendetta again the offspring of any mixed combination, including those with a Bereft parent.

Having yet to finish her first full year of life, Vic couldn't possibly threaten the Outcast, but he would not wait for her to grow up.

Jack may not even know it yet, but the instant they move Marina to a soulstone, his master will kill Vic.

"Give me the Teleportation scroll," says Marina. Her energy levels dip dangerously, but she hides it by leaning on the crib.

Jack sends her a measuring look.

"I'm not going anywhere while you have my daughter," she reminds him. "I want Raelyn to hold it so she can escape as soon as she wakes up."

Are you going to tell me the deal's changed yet?

Her brother's stillness says he is listening to his master. Finally, he hands her a scroll.

Guess not.

She confirms it's a Teleportation scroll.

Not quite done untangling Raelyn from the soulstone, Marina's content to continue the deception. Reluctantly leaving Vic's crib, she slowly crosses over to Raelyn and sits beside her.

She has avoided spending a lot of time next to her friend because she wanted to avoid drawing the Outcast's attention to her. But this last part must be done quickly, which requires direct contact.

A soft brown blanket lies bundled under Raelyn's head as a pillow. A heavier blue blanket has been draped over most of her body. Her arms lay atop the blanket.

Slipping the Teleportation scroll under Raelyn's right hand, Marina lifts the young woman's left hand to her chest. Then, she bows her head as if to pray and primes the scroll. By the time she's close to finishing, fatigue makes every limb feel heavy. She presses on, working even faster to direct bits of Raelyn's spirit and soul from the stone back into her body and bind them in place.

A short time later, Marina silently finishes the work that took her hours to accomplish. It should have been impossible, but the Gift for transferring energy makes it doable. Jack had wanted her to draw lifeforce in, but instead she's been directing energy out in three directions: Raelyn, the soulstone, and Vic.

Jack wanders back to the baby's crib.

Stop her!

The shout explodes in her head like it's coming from everywhere. A physical shock shakes the sand and makes the ruins groan around them.

Raelyn's eyes fly open.

Marina drops the young woman's hand and scoots back, grinning triumphantly.

Raelyn vanishes.

The blue blanket settles to the sand. With nothing holding it in a ball, the brown blanket spreads out.

Hauling herself back further, Marina leans listlessly against the wall.

What do you think you've accomplished? I have other servants who can kill her.

Marina doesn't answer the rant aloud.

She's away from you. She has a chance.

Jackson, kill the child and move Marina to the soulstone quickly. Summon the undead.

"Can't ... kill her." Marina rallies her strength to explain. "Without ... one of us. Daniel ... won't help."

Another boom sounds and the ground rumbles. A heavy chunk

of something crashes down a dozen paces away, sending up a spray of sand and small rocks that showers down on Marina.

"What's wrong, Master?"

Hold on the summoning. She's right. She's dying. She gave the Healer most of her remaining strength.

The Dark Man's thought rings with disgust.

Return the crib and chairs. Move anything you want to keep. Destroy the rest.

Jack plucks Vic out of the crib and follows the instructions. The privacy screen had already been moved aside once Marina didn't need it anymore. It disappears along with the other furniture and even the blankets conjured for Raelyn.

Chain Marina's wrist so she cannot escape. Then give her the child and break the temple seal. We must handle this a different way.

"You would have lived," Jack says, placing Vic into Marina's arms.

She doesn't fight him when he lifts her left hand and snaps the metal cuff around her wrist. Her eyes stay locked on her daughter's face.

"But she would not," Marina explains.

You have bought her mere days. When I have the artifact, I will kill your child and the huntsman and your Healer friend for good measure.

"Should I use the soulstone now?" asks Jack.

Don't bother. She's not strong enough to survive the transfer.

"What about the child?" Jack presses.

Also too weak. We must rely on the huntsman's skills and simpler spells to sustain the child. Magic that strong would kill her, and your sister is right again. We need at least one of them to control the huntsman. She has volunteered her daughter for that task.

I'm sorry, Vic. It was you or me, and I'm not strong enough to live without you.

Transfer me to the prisoner. Then summon the undead and disappear.

"Won't that risk killing them both?" Jack wonders.

I will control them. As soon as Marina is wounded, the huntsman will come and deal with the rest. You cannot be anywhere near here when that happens.

"Jack. Don't … do this. Don't … serve him."

He has no choice. My power flows through him. He must serve me.

Jack touches the prisoner's left shoulder.

A sustained shout fills the arena.

Marina wants to look away but can't.

The body slumps before bracing its feet and pulling forward. The chains pop free of the wall. Once again, the eyes glow green. Next, the corpse snaps the wrist manacles apart.

"Carry on," says the Dark Man with an airy wave.

A snap brings a scroll to Jack's hand. With great ceremony, he reads the words on the scroll.

One of the two bodies twitches.

Marina buries her face in the white wrap containing Vic.

"That won't do." The Dark Man makes a mocking noise with his borrowed throat. "Come, child, enjoy the show."

Pain pierces Marina's head until she lifts her eyes and watches the two Arkonai bodies reanimate. Once on their feet, they try to amble away.

"It seems our friends came without weapons. Give them some."

Jack conjures a variety of swords and blunt objects and waits for the new zombies to select something, then returns the unused weapons to wherever he pulled them from in the first place.

"I will finish our task. You may go."

Opening the Veil, Jack bows briefly to Marina then conjures himself elsewhere.

The undead slowly move closer.

One drops to a knee before Marina and picks up her right hand in a courtly gesture.

She transfers Vic to her left hand, rattling the chain connecting her to the wall.

"Would you like to know a secret?" inquires the Dark Man. "People believe a bite must be involved for the turning, but as long as my will prevails, any contact will do."

The corpse delicately kisses the back of Marina's right hand before reaching for Vic.

"No!" Panic gives Marina new strength. She shoves the corpse hard with her right hand then wraps both arms tightly around her baby, curling into a ball around her to offer the most protection.

Hands pin her in place while more hands pry Vic lose.

Vic!

"Hush. You can have her back shortly."

Everything in Marina screams to leap up and fight, but an oppressive presence paralyzes her.

Her mind spits out a long series of pleas and denials.

"We must make this look genuine."

After carefully extracting Vic's right arm from the white wrap, the corpse kisses her hand next to the wrist. Vic wakes with a scream as a bite wound appears.

Pain radiating from her own wrist draws Marina's attention down to where a similar wound appears.

One of the corpses places Vic on the sand next to Marina.

The baby wails until the Dark Man puts her into another deep sleep.

Desperate, Marina concentrates her magical effort on her daughter. Sharp pain strikes her head, chest, stomach, and limbs as the Destroyer Gifts strain to contain the disease set loose in her body. She directs the magic to Vic.

"Are you sure you want to do that?" asks the Dark Man. "The effort will kill you, and I'll just have to hurt her again."

Realizing he will carry out the threat, Marina changes tactics. Instead of seeking to destroy the disease, she tries to contain it, confining it to Vic's right hand.

"Much better. I knew I could count on your aid."

Drawing near, the Dark Man conjures a dagger.

"This looks very familiar." He smooths some of her hair and pushes until she's lying on her back. "No, not the same."

Lifting together, the Arkonai corpses prop Marina against the stone wall. One releases her wrist from the chain.

"Still different, but much closer," the Dark Man babbles. "This is how your sister looked before I killed her. She died so I could get to you. Having a pesky Minder connected to you would have ruined everything. Dear Jack was right. You didn't have to die this way. I had every intention of returning your soul, but I suppose this is more fitting."

Tears slip out.

"Don't be sad. You'll be with Gabriella soon, if she made it through the Darklands. They're becoming increasingly dangerous to cross." He rests a hand on her left cheek. "I would love to prolong this, but we need to ensure that Victoria's father makes it here in time to save her."

Epilogue:
The Dark Man's Gift

Combat Arena, Lower Level of the Earth Temple Ruins
Same day (Four days after Shadow's disappearance)
(Christa's twins are almost seven years old)
Before Daniel can officially refuse to lay down his weapon, he feels a sharp tug on his spirit.

Marina!

Following the feeling, Daniel teleports, appearing two paces away from his wife.

Vic lies next to her, still and silent.

A noise somewhere between a challenge and a moan hits his senses a split-second later. Ducking, Daniel spins and swings the greatsword. The weapon slams solidly into a man's arm, eliciting no more than a grunt. The man collapses but not from Daniel's strike. The slashed arm shows barely a trickle of blood.

Another man staggers toward him then groans and drops to his hands and knees. This time, Daniel looks closer. The man's head leans at a strange angle. A horrible realization washes over Daniel as he stares from one man to the other. Their clothes identify them as huntsmen, but their graceless movements tell him they're dead. Disgust, fear, and outrage roil around inside Daniel.

"Forgive me," calls a male voice from behind Daniel.

Bringing the sword up to a defensive position, Daniel whirls to face the new threat.

"I had not expected your response to be so prompt." A third

corpse addresses him in a deliberate, cordial manner. A gaping hole in his shirt near the right shoulder displays the cause of death. "Thank you for coming. You have many questions, but your wife and daughter are dying. Allow me to give you a gift before I explain your situation."

"Who are you?"

"I am the Dark Man."

Dark Man?

Daniel's head throbs, and his heart simply can't absorb the horrific events unfolding rapidly. He knows the name should mean something to him, but his emotions have shut down.

"What happened?" Daniel cautiously steps toward Marina and Victoria, keeping the sword trained on the undead man.

"Do you really wish to spend Marina's last moments questioning me?"

The query hits Daniel hard. His arms ache from holding the heavy sword. Strength drains rapidly from his arms. The sword tips toward the ground.

"You have impressive will, Daniel, but this form is beyond the threat of that sword. Put it back in the Veil and accept my gift."

Knowing the corpse speaks at least some truth, Daniel follows the advice and straightens with as much dignity as he can muster.

"May I go to them?" he asks.

"That is part of my gift to you." The Dark Man waves at Marina and Victoria as if presenting them.

Sweeping Victoria off the ground, Daniel examines her closely.

"She's alive, for now," says the Dark Man.

Daniel doesn't believe the spirit until he feels Victoria's tiny body move with her next breath.

"To receive the next part of the gift, you must let my spirit connect to yours." The corpse holds out a hand, palm up.

Daniel stares at it. Letting an unknown spirit enter him seems like a very bad idea.

The Dark Man smiles.

"It will be a temporary arrangement, I assure you, but you do not possess the magical abilities to move your family to safety or lend Marina the strength to survive such a journey."

The ground rumbles, shaking the temple.

Daniel looks to Marina for a sign, but her eyes have fallen shut. He looks to Victoria and again finds no answers.

"I also need your permission to transfer vitality to your wife."

"Yes." The answer comes instantly. Reaching out, Daniel grabs the proffered hand.

Pain enters at his fingers and travels quickly up his arm, spreads through his chest, and disappears. His eyes widen as every sense becomes sharper. The thud of the previous host's body echoes in Daniel's skull. A second of silence is followed by the faint rustling of settling rocks and dust. His eyes spot individual grains of sand clinging to Marina's cloak and dried blood on the stone walls behind her. A large bloodstain covers her left side, but her position hides the wound. The scent of mold, decay, and fresh blood assails him. A surge of energy makes him feel invincible.

Touch Marina, and I will see to the transfer.

Daniel shudders at the voice booming through his head. Nevertheless, he follows the instruction. As soon as he takes Marina's hand, Daniel feels his energy level dropping. He quickly sits down and cradles Victoria closer, lest he drop her.

The energy stops flowing from him.

"Please, continue," Daniel pleads.

We have only staved off death. It will come for her.

Daniel squeezes his wife's hand fiercely, trying to imagine life-giving magic flowing to her.

He feels no change, but when he dares to look again, they're no longer in a sandy pit surrounded by stone.

They're home.

Instead of leaning against a rough, bloodstained wall, Marina's head and shoulders rest against their bed.

Daniel's acute hearing picks up the subtle shifting of men's feet in the next room.

Do not worry about them. They will not interfere. Say your farewell.

Still cradling Victoria with his left arm, Daniel lays his other hand on Marina's face.

Her deep blue eyes open and meet his.

"Love you." Her words are low and labored but clear in the stillness. "Give Vic ... last gift."

"Love you too. Stay with me!" Daniel's composure slips. Tears blur his vision. He angrily dashes them away, furious that they're marring his last moments with Marina.

She tries to smile but can't quite manage it. Her eyes drift shut, and her head leans back against the bed.

171

Daniel rubs his thumb across her cheek, catching a warm tear. Grief builds in and around him, but shock holds it off.

"What did she mean?" he asks the dark spirit dwelling inside.

She wants you to take the last scraps of her lifeforce and use it to bolster the child's defenses.

"Do it." Daniel withdraws his hand from Marina to bring Victoria closer to her.

Outside my area of expertise. Strength is universal. Healing and protection spells are Light magic. You will have to ask the Lady for her blessing to accomplish it.

Daniel's heart cries out for a miracle.

Protect my daughter! Drive the disease away. Free her. Save her. Please. I need a miracle.

He grips Vic's tiny hand.

A sigh escapes Marina. Her eyes meet his once more before closing. Her head slumps toward her right shoulder.

When he reaches for Marina, Daniel senses nothing. His arms tremble, and he has to concentrate on not dropping Victoria. Shifting his grip on the baby, he cups Marina's face with his left hand. His fingers touch warm flesh, but his Seeker Gifts find only an empty shell. Tears blur his vision and fall onto the baby's white wrap. His breaths come in gasps between stabbing sensations of loss.

Marina's last gift has been delivered. Draw strength from that.

Daniel doesn't see anything change in his daughter, but he feels the shift in Victoria's spirit.

She's stronger now.

This is temporary. If you want to save your daughter's life, you must bring me the magic bracers. They are an artifact of Light I can use to cure her.

"How do I find them?" Externally, he sounds calm, but internally, Daniel feels rage rising.

You are a Seeker blessed by the Lady. Ask her. She will show you where to find them. You will bring them to me. Victoria will stay with the men to ensure this.

"I'm not leaving her with you or with anybody you choose." Daniel pulls the baby in and cradles her protectively.

A quest is no place for a child.

Daniel studies his daughter. Everything about her is perfect, except an angry wound on her right wrist. It looks like a bite mark, but dark magic surrounds and infects the wound. It's contained but not cured.

Vic.

Marina always insisted on shortening her name.

"If you want my help, she's coming," Daniel declares. He glares around the room, having nowhere to direct his anger since the spirit still dwells within him.

The spirit stays quiet.

Daniel experiences a fluttering in his stomach, indicating the spirit's unease with the change.

Take the men with you. The journey could be dangerous.

"I'll choose my own companions," Daniel argues.

I need a guarantee of your cooperation.

"You know I want to save my daughter," says Daniel. "If these bracers can do that, I will find them."

Hold please.

The order confuses Daniel.

A faint pop sounds.

His Seeker senses tell him the three presences in the next room have gone away.

A few seconds later, another pop sounds.

Daniel picks up four presences. Heart in his throat, he leaps up and dashes into the main room.

Three men form a semi-circle around a kneeling woman. Her head is angled downward, so he can't see a face past the long blond hair. Nevertheless, the presence is familiar.

Looking up, Raelyn stares solemnly at Daniel.

"I'm coming."

Daniel's head shakes.

The Healer has agreed to be my guarantee. In one of Marina's pockets you will find a soulstone.

"You're not putting her in it," says Daniel. He holds Vic in one arm in case he needs to draw a weapon soon.

She was in it until recently, but that is not the current plan. The Healer has placed her life in my hands. I will transfer a small piece of my essence into the soulstone. You will keep it with you at all times, so I can monitor your progress. If you fail to deliver the bracers, I will kill her and send assassins for everyone you and Marina ever held dear.

Pulling up the sleeves of her dress, Raelyn holds out her hands.

A faint red line appears on both of her wrists then fades away. She cups her hands together then unfolds them, revealing a large pitch black, smooth stone.

The Dark Man's spirit leaves Daniel, forming a smokey black mist that flows into the soulstone. A black leather cord appears, running through the stone, which shrinks until it's no bigger than Vic's palm.

Without a word, the three men file out.

Raelyn starts to rise.

Daniel helps her with his free hand.

"Why do you want to come with me?" Daniel's dry throat barely surrenders the question.

"You hold the reason why," Raelyn replies. Letting go of his hand, she slowly ties off the soulstone necklace and loops it into place. "Now that the Dark Man has retreated, we can speak openly. I've had strange dreams lately. There's a chance your daughter is the Lady's Chosen Redeemer. True or not, it's a possibility worth fighting for."

"But will he save her if we give him the bracers?"

Raelyn's look condemns Daniel's question as stupid.

"Of course not, we're giving them to Vic."

"You'll die."

"I was dead an hour ago." Raelyn frowns and lowers her voice. "Don't remember much besides Marina working tirelessly to revive me, so if I can help save her daughter, I'm doing it."

"Marina's dead," Daniel whispers. He glances back toward the bedroom. "In there."

"I know. It's written all over you." Tears fall, but Raelyn squares her shoulders. "What do you need from me? I can watch Vic so you have time to make arrangements, or I can call her mother and brother." Her eyes cloud with concern. "Will the funeral rites be Arkonai or Saroth?"

Burial or burning?

"Both," Daniel answers honestly. "She belonged to both worlds and would be the first to argue that people are people, only the stupid ones make distinctions based on magic schools."

The grief weighs heavily upon Daniel. He stands frozen, not sure how to form more thoughts or words.

Raelyn turns him around and pushes.

"Go be with her," she orders. "I will send the proper messages."

Daniel stumbles into the bedroom. His wife's body still lies crumpled next to the bed.

"Help me."

The whispered request brings Raelyn to Daniel's side. While placing Vic in her crib, Daniel idly notes it's been moved, but he doesn't care.

Together, he and Raelyn lift Marina off the floor and place her carefully on the bed. Next, Raelyn fetches some wet cloths for him before leaving to make the necessary notifications.

Daniel washes dust, dirt, blood, sweat, and tears from his wife's face, arms, and hands. He cleans and binds the wound on Marina's side and places her hands across her stomach. Finally, he retrieves Vic from the crib and holds her, letting tears form and fall. Daniel has never experienced this kind of devastating pain, something simultaneously cold, hot, numbing, stabbing, and crushing, but he draws the strength to keep breathing by watching his daughter sleep in his arms.

THE END

Thank You for Reading:

This probably shouldn't be your first Aeris tale, seeing as it's smack in the middle of a trilogy. If you need to catch up, check out *River's Edge Ransom* (a short story) and *The Huntsman and the Healer*. The adventure continues in *The Lady's Grace*. Be sure to read the original Redeemer Chronicles series, which includes *Awakening*, *The Holy War*, and *Reclaim the Darklands*.

Aeris stories in order: *River's Edge Ransom, The Huntsman and the Healer, The Dark Man's Wrath, The Lady's Grace, Awakening, The Holy War,* and *Reclaim the Darklands.*

Please visit my website: **www.juliecgilbert.com**. Check out the audiobooks. They have fantastic narrators. Or try another paperback.

I would love to connect via email:
devyaschildren@gmail.com

www.ingramcontent.com/pod-product-compliance
Lightning Source LLC
Chambersburg PA
CBHW061209170626
46809CB00003B/1303